Three Postcards from A...

By Shanna Yetman

Dad:

Remember Wal-Drug? I'm writing from that general store with the ice cream parlor. That mechanical T-Rex is still here, brandishing its teeth! The kids LOVE it. We sat for a long time, listening. Overcrowded and kitschy, you'd say, but we always left well stocked. Reminds me of our old road trips. Almost no road, mostly dust. Asphalt goes quickly when there's this much foot traffic. We are now part of that steady stream of migrants leaving the coasts and heading inland. We've been pushed out. Delaware is a launch site.

What will we do?

Remember to look up. The sky is an exquisite purple-turquoise-ceylon-green. They've begun to use a rainbow of colors for the sulfites they spray into the stratosphere.

There's a succulent smell in the air and daytime is like dusk, even the animals walk with us.

    Love from your nomads (Rosie, Ava & Emmett)

Hey G-Pops!

Mom's making me write these stupid postcards before we rest. She says it'll help me with my writing skillz. (She's going to read that and make me correct it— I'm keeping it!) My writing skillz are fine if you're worried. I'm keeping a journal and documenting those wild buttes (butts?) that surround us. Like a layer cake. Deposition and Erosion. That's what created this place.

I love the bright yellow mounds. FACT: It's fossilized soil. FACT: These lands BE BAD and OLD (like you).

The whole world is a shimmering fog, and the air feels like a cotton ball. That's cool. And, it's a little cooler! So? Go humanity! Anyway, I miss my video games!

Mom says we're walking towards you. Will we ever find you? If we do, will we give you these postcards? Is that how this works?

    Love, Ava

Grandpa:

We'll never find you, which means no one will ever read this, so I'll say whatever I want. It's still hot and NOW there's no sun. Though, I see a faint glimmer of it sometimes. Is that good or bad? They're calling this SUN DIMMING. They've got plans to spray the earth every three months for the next five years. YOU KNOW this (if you're alive). It's wild. But also, beautiful? It feels like we're on another Earth. One we've created and now spray painted? Tagged Earth2.0? People worry about what rainfall will be like and how the plants will grow, but I worry about forgetting.

Who will we be when we can't remember how bright sunlight feels on our skin or what it's like to watch white clouds roll through a (real) blue sky?

I hear you in my head. I know what you're gonna ask. So, here goes nothing: I'm thankful for the days when they blanket the world in a deep green mist. The sky looks killer then.

    Emmett

A MAGAZINE OF SCIENCE & FANTASY FICTION
DREAMFORGE

About This Issue

In Issue 12, we look forward to the brighter and more balanced future technology can bring, while acknowledging that humanity is the business of our hearts, and that regardless of the place or time, we find the true strength of our species in our shared ability to learn from each other, to transform difference into unity, and to create a world where everyone belongs.

Three Postcards from Another Earth 1
  By Shanna Yetman
Editor's Notes: Looking Back and Looking Forward 3
  By Jane Noel
Write the Future You Want to Live In 4
  An Essay By Ana Sun
A Bowl of Soup on the 87th Floor 8
  By Kai Holmwood
Count It An Anchor 13
  By Taffy Lamba
Another Day on the Orbital Ranch 18
  By David Hankins, Illustrated by Jake Niehl
Petrichor 23
  By Richard A Shury
Like Stars Daring To Shine 24
  Reprint By Somto Ihezue
The Rainmakers 28
  Reprint By Megan M. Davies-Ostrom
Lost in Intuition 34
  By Amara Mesnik
It's Time To Discover *WRITERS OF THE FUTURE VOLUME 39* 39
  By Dr. Lee Carrol
The Park 42
  By Teresa Milbrodt
A Language Older Than Words 46
  By Andrew Giffen
Asylum 51
  By Gretchen Tessmer
Thread 52
  By Bret Nelson
The Jewel of the Waves, the Diadem of the Sky 58
  By Jared Oliver Adams
Flybys, Launch Windows, and Selfies with the Earth and Moon 64
  By Robert E. Harpold
A Special Thank You to our Tier 3 Patrons 67
Thank You 68

DreamForge Magazine
A Magazine of Science & Fantasy Fiction
www.DreamForgeMagazine.com

Publisher & Editor
Scot Noel

Graphic Design, Layout & Website
Jane Noel

Senior Advisor & Creative Consultant
Jane Lindskold

Editorial Assistants
Henry Gasko
Catherine Weaver

Copy Editor
Lois Yeager

Advertising
Advertising@DreamForgeMagazine.com

Customer Services
Subscriber@DreamForgeMagazine.com

Vol 4 Issue 12

DreamForge Magazine is published by DreamForge Press LLC, 2615 Detroit Street, Grapeville, PA 15634.

Stories are freely available online, however, if you'd like to support us with a subscription, visit us at www.DreamForgeMagazine.com. All income from subscriptions goes to purchase stories or art.

Access to online issues is available at Portal.DreamForgeMagazine.com. Subscribers also have access to MOBI, EPUB and PDF versions.

A printed version of DreamForge Magazine is available through Amazon Print on Demand.

Copyrights to stories and illustrations are the property of their creators. All rights reserved. Protection secured under the Universal Copyright Convention. Reproduction or use of editorial or graphic content without consent of the copyright holder is prohibited.

Submission: Please check our website for submission guidelines: www.dreamforgemagazine.com/call-for-submissions

CONNECTING DREAMERS – PAST AND FUTURE
IMAGINE • ENGAGE • INSPIRE

Looking Back and Looking Forward
By Jane Noel

As we are starting our fifth year of publication, we've been looking forward and looking back.

In May, we prepared for and launched our fifth Kickstarter campaign with the stretch goal of paying the pro-rate of 8 cents/word. We want to achieve and maintain that rate in the future as we continue to publish established authors and find, help, and publish new authors and new voices from around the world.

At DreamForge, we believe that we become what we imagine! So, all DreamForge stories engage readers with strong, empathetic characters and welcoming communities committed to positive outcomes. Our 2024 Mega Issue will take on the theme of "The Grand Uplift," where stories will focus on grand events and powerful movements that spark positive change, collective endeavors that elevate humanity, and a sense of shared purpose in communities working toward uplifting themselves and others. Stories for "The Grand Uplift" suggests an inspiring and momentous shift that benefits humanity, fostering a sense of hope, progress, and optimism.

So How Did We Get Here?

Well, back in 2018, Scot came up with the crazy idea to start a magazine. It started from conversations we had about the amount of dystopian and grimdark stories out in the world. (While we, too enjoy a good dystopia now and then, these darker stories, movies, games, etc. seemed to dominate the landscape.)

Scot grew up on the optimism of Star Trek and science fiction of the 50s and 60s. In many of these stories the community or the hero worked with technology to make the world a better place. Jane grew up on heroic fantasies like The Lord of the Rings where battles were fought to save the world.

We talked with our long-time friend and best-selling author Jane Lindskold about the idea, and she agreed to help. We knew it was a risky proposition and we knew it was a lot of work. (Although I'm not sure we really understood how much work!) We developed the theme and design of the magazine and created a logo and masthead.

We learned that the Nebula Awards were in Pittsburgh in May of 2018. It was right around our 20th Wedding Anniversary, and we decided our anniversary trip would be to go to the Nebulas. That really started our journey into the publishing industry, which we knew very little about.

When we first checked in at the Nebulas, they asked why we had come and we replied, "Well we're thinking about starting a magazine." They responded by setting up a welcome meeting with Scott Edelman because he has tremendous experience with magazines and in the industry overall. Over that weekend, we met with Neil Clarke from Clarkesworld, Scott Andrews from Beneath Ceaseless Skies, and Pablo Defedini, then with Fireside Magazine. By the end of the weekend, in a conversation with Scott Andrews, we remarked how amazing it was that everyone was so open with information about their businesses and trying to help us avoid common problems. He said, "That guy over there (pointing at Neil Clarke), helped me get started. I'll help you get started. You help the next person get started. That's how it works."

We've Met Many Wonderful People

Through the years, we've met wonderful people, digitally and in person.

Our very first Patreon supporter, Jamie Munroe is from Australia. He became our first editorial assistant and helped us build our outstanding corps of First Line Readers. We count him as a friend.

And those first line readers are integral to helping us select the very best stories for each issue. They freely dedicate their time and offer honest opinions to help Scot in so many ways. We truly appreciate all they do.

We've worked with Angela Yuriko Smith, publisher of Space & Time Magazine, on several initiatives. (Angela took over the reins on Space & Time just about the same time we started DreamForge.) This led to the publication of Worlds of Light and Darkness from Uproar Books where selected stories from each magazine were collected in a very well-received anthology.

We've become great friends with Wulf Moon. Moon won Writers of the Future during our first year of publication– when we sent magazines to the winners. He knew right away that he wanted to help and support the endeavor. As he grew in his career as author, he developed his Super Secrets of Writing and with his "pay it forward" attitude has shared those secrets with many new writers who have come together to form his Wulf Pack. Since 2021, Moon has written an article on writing for almost every issue of our digital version, DreamForge Anvil. They are a wonderful resource for writers and highly entertaining.

A couple of years back, as a Kickstarter reward, we offered some videos to help writers learn their craft. As an editor, Scot saw many common mistakes in stories. Combine that with Wulf Moon's expertise, we had some very successful webinars. It was such fun to get writers together for conversations, that we came up with the idea to create DreamCasters.

DreamCasters support us through Kickstarter or Patreon. In turn we have monthly meetings and a Discord server where we discuss the craft and business of writing. We've had wonderful guests including authors like Marie Vibbert, Bruce McAllister, Jane Lindskold, and Mary Robinette Kowal. Emily Mah Tippets came to talk about e-publishing, Crystal Crawford joined us to talk about the Kindle Vella Platform and literary agent Rick Lewis from Martin Literary Management discussed how to query and find an agent. The DreamCasters are awesome!

Just this past April, Scot was invited to the Writers and Illustrators of the Future in Hollywood California. (And I went along too.) As a former winner (Volume 6 in 1990), Scot was asked to do a presentation to the authors about writing for magazines and I talked to the illustrators. It was a wonderful experience where we got to meet some of our digital friends in person (including John Goodwin, the President of Galaxy Press, Wulf Moon, our current Editorial Assistant Catherine Weaver, and Dreamcasters (and WOTF winners) including David Hankins and Brittany Rainsdon – as well as meeting many other wonderful people who will become friends in in the future.

Where Are We Going?

So here we are, starting our fifth year. We've had more great experiences and met more wonderful people than we ever could have anticipated. We have authors, friends, and supporters from all around the world– like-minded people who don't think the world is going to hell in a handbasket, people who do see good in the world, and are optimistic that communities can come together and envision something more for humanity.

We don't know where the future is going to take us, where it will take DreamForge Magazine. Still, we hope to let some little mark on the world and inspire others to see our grand vision: That the human adventure is just beginning.

WRITE THE FUTURE YOU WANT TO LIVE IN

AN ESSAY BY ANA SUN

Take a moment: fast forward your imagination into the future, let's say a hundred years from now, maybe two hundred. Now picture yourself in it. Who are you in that world? What would you be doing? What surrounds you— what sights, sounds?

I don't find it easy to dream up a world beyond just an extension of our current reality— a world seemingly full of injustices, where our man-made climate emergency has likely set off a chain of irreparable disasters. And yet I very much want to believe that, as a species, we have the ingenuity and capability to turn things around and construct a better world. In fact, we already have so many potential solutions to decarbonize, to decouple ourselves from extractive practices upon our planet and the continual exploitation of fellow human beings. So, what are we up against? A lack of political will, a lack of imagination on how to shift away from the status quo.

A bit over a year ago, I had the chance to ask the author who coined the term *cyberpunk*, Bruce Bethke. I asked him: do we live in a cyberpunk world? "Absolutely", he said without hesitation, and immediately added, "I wasn't pessimistic enough."

Does this mean that concocting dreams and writing stories of hope constitutes nothing but self-indulgent folly?

There's a pretty good chance you've come across the oft-quoted anecdote on how the Star Trek communicator inspired the flip phone. This is usually preceded or followed by an assertion: because of this, speculative fiction has a place; we should keep writing it because it has a genuine impact on the world. Turns out the second claim has support of some scientific evidence, but there's more to the story— I'll come back to that.

Until recently, I merely thought of this as a myth, something belonging squarely in the correlation-not-causation bucket. Fiction? Influence the world? Hah. Pull the other one, it's got bells on.

But I can pinpoint the precise moment I changed my mind.

SPECULATIVE FICTION'S HANDPRINT

The time: late 2020. The place: behind my computer monitor, in my cold, under-insulated home office with a drafty excuse for a window, not unlike many such energy-inefficient Victorian conversions in Britain. Temporarily untethered from the physical world by the pandemic, many events lowered or waived registration fees as they moved online. Still suffering from long Covid and with work contracts on hold, I took the chance to attend things that were off my normally well-beaten path.

The event in question: an academic conference on social robotics, a topic I knew next to nothing about. Listening to academics and engineers explain their work, I was surprised at how often fictional robots were referred to. Like, how fictional robots had been used as part of a study on human-robot interaction because it approximated a baseline on human expectations. Turns out Wall-E has a bit more influence than HAL 2000 on engineers working on our latest robots. Heartening to know that a little romantic, environmental-themed robot has a slight edge over a homicidal AI. It also seems positive or utopian fiction plays a part (Mubin et al., 2019):

Our results also showed that sci-fi does not only have a relation with the development of technology but even more elaborate is its role as a medium of discourse, discussion, and communication. Researchers are most likely easily attracted to the utopian visions of sci-fi and the dystopian views are at times neglected, particularly when it comes to state-of-the-art research. In summary, science fiction has an important and significant relationship with the development of technology and one that we would expect to continue to evolve.

Later, I stumbled across an entire book dedicated to analysing interaction design from science fiction.

Positive visions don't just affect scientists, designers and engineers. A growing body of research shows how positive fictional role models have the capacity to empower and to change attitudes on how we might react to the climate emergency. This is especially true of stories that highlight solutions, according to one such ecopsychology study by Prof. Denise Baden:

Results indicated that for the vast majority, solution-focused stories were deemed to be most effective in motivating pro-environmental behaviours (PEBs). Role models were especially effective when they were relatable to and carrying out actions that the reader could easily imitate.

While we know systemic change is going to be necessary —individual actions count for only a small part— let's not forget that if many individuals are mobilized, we become a collective. A community spurred to action, we have the power to drive change.

I'd implied earlier that the Star Trek communicator may not have been the only influence on the flip phone. In the first few minutes of a 2015 interview, Marty Cooper, credited for inventing the mobile or cell phone, cited that his inspiration was more likely to have been Dick Tracy's wrist two-way radio conceived in the comic strip in 1946. Our smartwatches today possibly also descended from that legacy. So while it wasn't the piece of fiction we'd come to believe, it was still fiction that inspired the modern portable phone. The development might have just taken a bit longer than we'd expected; real-world technology takes time— it isn't quite magic.

Without narratives or provocations to play out what our world could look like, we'd remain trapped within the confines of corporate imagination— or lack thereof. We are already stuck on recycling ideas because new ideas are unknown territories much less monetizable than nostalgia. The decision whether a certain technology lives, dies, or thrives rests on capitalistic agents out to make a buck, or several million in the markets— regardless of clear benefits to humans and our planet, and historically, in spite of threats to human safety. Hello and goodbye, repairable electronics. Social media? See aforementioned comment on safety. Within a decade of its invention, privately-owned social media has begun resembling a dystopian experiment.

But from the precursor of social media and the communities behind early personal-blogging platforms, Wikipedia emerged, as did Creative Commons, a legal framework to explicitly enable the sharing of intellectual property so that creators can choose to allow derivatives of their works, enabling collective creativity to blossom. Concepts like Patreon, Kickstarter, all percolated from "crowdsourcing", harnessing the power behind communities to support independent art and projects for which there might be little or no top-down funding— projects that might have otherwise never seen the light of day.

SOLARPUNK AS COUNTERCULTURE ZEITGEIST

In 2018, when I stumbled upon the Mastodon community sunbeam.city, I recognized a composite of concepts: grassroot movements openly sharing knowledge, open governance, the championing of the commons, the strife for inclusivity and civil rights— a timely collision of 1960s counterculture with social technology. Only this time, the backdrop is a major shift in discourse on how we might deal with —or live with— the climate emergency, finally in the same breath as its relationship to inequalities and social injustices surfaced by colonization, unfettered capitalism and neoliberal ideals.

Since its first known description in 2008, a lot has been written and studied about solarpunk as a literary, artistic and activist movement. One of the speediest ways to grasp solarpunk principles is through a collectively authored manifesto housed at Regenerative Design. The Wikipedia entry on solarpunk also happens to be a good place to begin. The free encyclopaedia itself embodies solarpunk values as a volunteer-run, non-profit organisation, running on open-source software dedicated to documenting society's best version of truth through open collaboration. It's not without its faults, but it has become a largely resilient ecosystem that enables readjustments of long-standing biases.

If you're reading this online, it's thanks to technology built on open standards, developed by many hands who also fought against corporate attempts to dominate the market. At least two-thirds of the World Wide Web runs on open-source web servers, so there's also a high chance you have loaded a page today that depended on the effort of hundreds, if not thousands of people.

Solarpunk is already here and has been for a long time— it just had different names.

Old hands in the solarpunk community such as Jay Springett called solarpunk a "memetic engine" and Phoebe Wagner, a co-editor of one of the first solarpunk anthologies *Sunvault: Stories of Solarpunk and Eco-Speculation*, described how there's a trend towards letting people define what solarpunk means to them. In other words, solarpunk has become a loosely defined "container" of principles that everyone would have the freedom to interpret for themselves. This makes a certain sense: solarpunk stories present a positive progression of the now into the future, and a future that includes all of us on this planet requires nuanced and diverse narratives. In practice, how solarpunk principles influence your locale may be different from mine.

Quite often I find myself having to qualify it to friends and peers in the science-fiction and fantasy writing community: it's not just about gardening stories, sunshine and rainbows. At its core, solarpunk is political discourse: the acknowledgement that humans are part of this ecosystem we call Earth. My personal working definition is that solarpunk narratives show a potentially viable future where the decentralization of power —literally, and metaphorically— allows us to be accountable for how we live in harmony with those around us, humans or otherwise.

Again, many of these underlying ideas within literature considered "solarpunk" are not new. Core readings include Ursula K. Leguin's 1974 novel "The Dispossessed", Ernest Callenbach's "Ecotopia", or Murray Bookchin's numerous treatises. Apart from the books read by Goodreads Solarpunk group, various people in the community have compiled collective reading lists.

Francesco Verso, award-winning author and editor of Future Fiction, described to me two kinds of solarpunk stories he has read: (1) stories by the more privileged, who can "optimistically imagine hopeful narratives that include cultivating past values of purity and innocence", where they've survived a catastrophe or an apocalypse so they must rebuild a new civilization; (2) stories by the non-privileged who "cannot look at the past without being horrified, and thus must turn to the future to build their identity and space of existence"— where the catastrophe is happening now and they must fight to overcome it, to get away from the experience of daily apocalypses. And by that, he means things as basic as human rights, education and healthcare.

Sunshine and rainbows? It depends on who you ask.

WRITING HOPE DOES NOT DISMISS DESPAIR

Some time ago, in the middle of a casual discussion at a convention, I found myself describing how challenging it is for the people of my hometown in Asia to arrive at solarpunk futures. We still aspire to progress as defined for us by the Global North because there doesn't seem to be an alternative. Our post-colonial past made it ripe for corruption at the highest level of government. Our stories tend to be horror or petty dramas. We spend most of our time re-treading the past, trying to rediscover who we were, reinventing who we thought we might have been.

Choosing to write from a place of hope doesn't mean that it's a dismissal of the challenging realities we face. As I write, over 7.2 million people in my adopted country are struggling with essentials like food or adequate clothing, and over 3 million households cannot afford to heat their homes. Yes, I currently live in the United Kingdom— technically, the Global North. We are witnessing decades of failed government policies based on neoliberal doctrine, and we're finding out the hard way how trickle down economics don't work. But in the hour of need, communities look after each other: all across the UK, local councils, libraries, museums and community halls have created warm refuges for those who struggle. Not so long ago, like many other places around the world, we witnessed neighbours self-organize into mutual aid groups during Covid-19.

Contrary to popular belief, according to Prof. Penny Spikins, there exists compelling evidence that the species from which we originated were kind and compassionate, all the way back to the Stone Age. In his book "Humankind," Rutger Bregman offers more recent examples, along with several explanations of why our compassionate nature can be corrupted by those in power. But one of his most compelling deep dives is the story of Kitty Genovese, whose brutal murder gave rise to the "bystander effect" because the press perpetuated the story that thirty-eight witnesses did nothing to help her. We learn how that single instance of unchallenged journalistic spin on human indifference (because, hey, stories of humans mistreating each other sell well) went on to bias the social narrative for five decades.

But you might be pleased to know: the bystander effect has finally been resoundingly disproved. The current statistics show that if you got into trouble, in 90% of the cases, someone would go out of their way to help you. It only took us fifty years to set the story straight, that we are not naturally horrible to each other—quite the opposite.

The sad fact: our brains are attracted to threats and fears, and it's precisely this weakness that's exploited by politicians, some of the press, and— well, anyone else who benefits from mutual distrust. Stories are like "flight simulators for the brain" (Health & Health 2007) and if we're not careful, we could train ourselves into less than desirable narratives. Marissa Lingen's excellent article "Beware the Lifeboat" has never been so spot on:

When we look into the faces of climate refugees, how we react will depend greatly on what responses to lifeboat problem stories we've internalized.

In fiction, we ought to be vigilant that it's not "cold equations" alone —as made famous by Tom Godwin's classic short story— that are responsible for tales of suffering; we as storytellers are the ones who create and post-rationalize those circumstances for which innocents could be mistreated, or worse, murdered.

Don't get me wrong; dystopia has its place. We need stories that remind us of how we got here so we retain the memory of our past mistakes and hardships; we need stories that examine the darker sides of our psyches. But fear comes easier than courage, hope takes emotional work. Without the will to drive narrative change and create visions for a better world, more people will continue to suffer, and we will continue to incorrectly justify that it's merely human nature. I cannot see how that is in any way desirable for a future I want to live in.

A LIVEABLE FUTURE AS A GENRE

When someone asks me about writing solarpunk— my first advice is to read what's already out there.

On a panel for Spectrum Writers London in 2021, Fabio Fernandez, who translated the first solarpunk anthology, described some stories he'd encountered as science fantasy which abides by Clarke's law (where "any sufficiently advanced technology is indistinguishable from magic"), some about smart solutions for everyday problems in the far future, or stories that are more immediate.

At the same event, Sarena Ullibari, who edited and published the canonical "Glass and Gardens" summer and winter anthologies, described how solarpunk stories could be a "genre" or a "mode"— the latter being stories which use solarpunk as a lens but may not show specific solutions. For example, you might have a romance or hard-boiled detective fiction in a solarpunk setting. Some solarpunk stories may address a problem and present a solution, but others show how people live in a future where a particular problem has been solved, and hand-wave over the details of how we got there. As editor-in-chief of World Weaver Press, as well as someone who read for Imagine 2200, she had a list of common issues she's seen with solarpunk stories. I scribbled extensive notes.

She suggests that authors:
- be aware of specific local impacts— understand climate change is different from other 20th century disasters (it won't be like a nuclear war)
- resist "blank slate stories" that focuses on rebuilding a future after a massive die-off (apocalypse) from pandemic, war, from ecological collapse
- imagine a trajectory forward from our present situation where most people and life forms survive
- refrain from making up random or impractical technology— look at architectural, material sciences: "what's niche which could be mainstream, what's conceptual now but could be reality soon"
- resist aesthetics that "looks" solarpunk, but in reality would have a high negative environmental impact because of the potential for greenwashing
- let go of the "utopic"— better futures do not mean perfect futures
- construct story conflicts that do not necessarily mean planetary life/death; quiet, small-scale or low personal stakes have a place in solarpunk stories.

While solarpunk encompasses a broad range, some core principles are handy to keep in mind. My favourite list of guidelines come from a podcast, a collaboration between James Tomasino and Paweł Ngei:
1. Community as Protagonist (No "Chosen One")
2. Infrastructure is Sexy (No simple solution)
3. Human/Environmental Context (Not Man vs Nature)

We could go a little further by honouring a variety of storytelling traditions. Vida Cruz, who won an Ignyte award for her non-fiction article "We are the Mountain: A Look at the Inactive Protagonist" has excellent guidance on ways to decolonize your fiction. We can imagine addressing the myriad of challenges as we transition in stages towards a better world.

But where to begin? Phoebe Wagner has spoken on several occasions how she looks to her immediate environment or community for inspiration. What issues do your communities face? What would a positive change look like?

Personally, I examined the fault lines in my own communities —such as having lore pitted against empirical science— which became the basis of the conflict in "Dandelion Brew". My story "La bibilothèque d'objets quotidiens" which closed the first volume of *The Librarian* anthology takes inspiration from a real-life library of things right in my town mashed up with a favourite Dr. Who episode. "The Scent of Green", in an upcoming anthology *Fight for the Future: Cyberpunk and Solarpunk Tales* by Android Press, explores the challenges of knowledge sharing if communities were autonomous, self-reliant but fragmented— ideas I borrowed from past experience in grassroots activism. Lately I've been challenging myself; every time I see a negative headline, I think: how can we turn this around?

Today, our economy is largely late-stage capitalist, especially in the Global North. Developing countries are forced to fall in line to pull their population out of post-colonial poverty, incurring massive carbon footprint driven by consumerist demands of the developed world, at the same time having better, energy-efficient technology priced out of reach. Corporations have a lot of power and are seldom held accountable for their actions— or their accounting. Wealthy countries ship their plastic waste to developing countries in Asia that have no capacity or technology to deal with it. We can't really know how much biodiversity we will lose because we don't actually have a clear idea of how many species exist. Estimates of yearly extinctions range between low estimates of two-hundred and two-thousand, to upper estimates between ten thousand and a hundred thousand species. Per year. You read that right.

Yet at COP27 in November 2022, despite finally agreeing on a loss and damage fund to help poorer countries affected by climate disasters, we couldn't agree on phasing down all fossil fuels. Most financial service institutions that have pledged to reach net zero are still investing heavily in fossil fuels.

Choosing hope is a difficult path, but no superhero is going to dash into save us. If we want a better world, we're going to have to make it ourselves. There's no shortage of problems to set our imaginations alight: how might a more egalitarian economy come to pass, and what struggles would we have to overcome to get there? What would society look like, if citizens ran their own power grids? What cuisines could we rediscover, if we honour sustainable food-growing practices and have more diverse crops?

While activists fight tirelessly to expose malpractices and shift the Overton window, policymakers push for concrete changes, engineers and designers develop feasible technology, we need narratives to show us that a better world is possible, and how we might get there. More than ever, we have a responsibility to forge new dreams, so that our grandchildren —and their grandchildren— can look forward to a world worth living in.

The digital version of this well-researched article in DreamForge Anvil 11 contains over fify links to references and supporting articles. You can find the digital version at https://bit.ly/df-write-the-future.

A Bowl of Soup
ON THE 87TH FLOOR
By Kai Holmwood

Mabel wrapped her hands around the steaming bowl of soup, soaking in some of its heat. The older she had grown, the harder it had become to stay warm, even with the solar-powered climate control designed to keep buildings comfortable for plants and people alike. She savored the feeling of the artisanal bowl in her hands. The inside was glazed in earthy greens, but the outside was rough clay. The herbaceous, verdant aroma of the soup contributed to the forestal effect.

Just as she was about to eat, the familiar voice of the system linked to the device wrapped around her right arm spoke:

ONE PERSON HAS ARRIVED. WELCOME, JUNIPER.

"Hello? Sorry, are you open? My LEAF said…" came a tentative voice from the attached dining area.

"One moment, please!" Mabel called through the door. She set her bowl down carefully, then walked from the back kitchen into the dining area, wiping her hands on her apron. "Sorry about that," she said to the young woman of maybe twenty-five years old waiting half-inside the front door. "Are you here to eat?"

Juniper nodded. "I've heard you make the best soup in Oakstead. Am I too early? I can come back later."

"I'm just slow to get going today, dear. Please, sit wherever you'd like." As Mabel spoke, she took the opportunity to observe the other woman more closely. Juniper's loose wrappings in shades of green and yellow hid neither her sinewy leanness nor her tentative, almost awkward way of moving.

With a grateful smile, Juniper sat at a window table. From there, nestled in its 87th-floor vantage point, Mabel's restaurant offered a view of the surrounding ecocity stretching toward sun and sky. Buildings clad in glittering solar glass, vibrant green spaces, and balconies shaded in vine. Down the bustling avenues, at a distance, the wilds beyond the city's boundaries faded into the horizon.

"Sorry, I couldn't find a menu on my LEAF," Juniper said with a pointed glance toward the device on her arm, identical to Mabel's in all but the final decorative details.

"No, dear, you wouldn't." Explaining to new diners why the Life and Environment Assistance and Facilitation System didn't show a menu always offered insight into their personalities. "You see, I make only one variety per day, and never the same thing twice. Otherwise, I'd get bored of my own creations."

"So, this is a once-in-a-lifetime experience twice over, then. Eating at your famous restaurant and eating a soup that will never exist again."

"I hope it will live up to expectations," Mabel said, then stepped into the kitchen and glanced longingly at her own meal. Well, it would just have to wait. She ladled a generous portion into another handmade bowl and carried it to the table, where she placed it in front of Juniper before garnishing it. "Now, before you begin, I have one request."

"What's that?"

"Each soup is a part of me that I'm sharing with you. If you're willing, would you share part of yourself with me too? It can be anything: how many siblings you have, your favorite flower, the dish that most reminds you of your childhood. Or, of course, nothing at all. It's an invitation, not an obligation."

Juniper let out a little laugh. "Let's see. My parents both worked in species restoration. That's why my dad named me for one of the trees that— well, that didn't make it through the Long Drought."

"I heard juniper used to grow all over this region," Mabel offered, as if in sympathy.

Juniper's face brightened. "You know of it?"

"They used to use its berries as a spice, and for a drink."

"Of course! Most people have to ask their LEAF."

"Well, decades of cooking will teach you a thing or two about flavorings, even long-extinct ones." Mabel glanced at Juniper's meal, still perfectly garnished and untouched.

Juniper's eyes followed Mabel's gaze, and she flushed. "I'm sorry, I'm talking too much and letting it get cold! Should I stir in the toppings, or eat it as it is?"

"That's up to you, dear."

Juniper's hand, holding her spoon, hesitated over the bowl—then she scooped up a bite and brought it to her mouth.

Mabel smiled. She had meant it, really, that guests were welcome to stir in the garnishes if they preferred, but it always made her happy to see someone eating as she had intended. After all, if she had wanted those components mixed in, she would have done so herself.

Without speaking, Juniper took a second bite, then a third, then a fourth. Mabel liked that, too. Far too many people let out appreciative "mmm"s and "yum"s the instant the soup hit their tongues, long before they had a chance to actually taste its nuances.

"This," Juniper said eventually, "is even better than I had heard. What is it, if I may ask?"

Mabel beamed. "I'm so glad, dear! It's a nettle, chickweed, and thyme soup puréed with pine nuts for creaminess, then finished with a marjoram, lemon zest, and toasted garlic gremolata and a drizzle of olive oil infused with preserved lemons. I think if I were to make this one again, I would add burdock."

"But you won't?"

"I might use this one as inspiration for another one someday, but it won't be the same."

The door swung open, and several of Mabel's regulars walked in together as the system, rather unnecessarily, announced their arrival.

THREE PEOPLE HAVE ARRIVED. WELCOME, TALIA, MONA, AND FINN.

"Would you excuse me?" Mabel set about preparing three bowls of soup. Something the young woman had said was tickling the back of her mind, and she knew it would pester her until she figured it out. She set down the three bowls in front of the familiar arrivals and chatted with them for a few minutes, but her thoughts were on the stranger.

Ah hah. There it was.

Mabel returned to the window table and peered at Juniper, who had half-finished her soup. "You aren't from Oakstead," she observed.

Juniper wiped her mouth with a linen napkin. "Why do you say that?"

"All the buildings here are named after trees and plants. Mostly living species, of course, but our Juniper Building was named in remembrance of what was lost. Everyone here has heard of junipers."

Juniper absently stirred the soup remaining in her bowl, mixing in the rest of the garnish. "You're right," she said eventually. "I'm not from Oakstead."

"I don't get many travelers here. Most of my customers are regulars."

"I see why you did the garnishes on top," Juniper said. "Stirring them into the soup dilutes their flavor and means every bite is the same. Leaving them on top adds some variation."

"Very well," Mabel laughed. "I won't pry, dear."

Juniper cast her a grateful smile. "Would it be too greedy if I asked for a second bowl?"

Mabel felt herself beaming. "Of course not! I'd never let a guest go hungry."

Five hours, forty-three guests, and sixty-two bowls of soup later, Mabel was ready to close shop. Juniper was still sitting at the window, gazing at nothing in particular with a faraway look in her eyes.

"Would you like one more bowl before you go?" Mabel said.

Juniper's attention shifted to Mabel, and the younger woman smiled. "Thank you, but no. I've taken too much of your time already. But could I come back tomorrow?"

The next day, Juniper traded her favorite color for a bowl of smoky tomato broth poured over blistered padron peppers, charred and chopped eggplant, and herbed couscous. The day after that, she spoke of the smell of a frosty night under the stars as she ate the rosemary, chard, sunchoke, and roasted chestnut soup finished with pink peppercorns and pear vinegar.

By the end of a week, Mabel found herself eating at the window with Juniper rather than rushing to finish her meal in the kitchen. At this rate, Mabel thought, Juniper would soon become part of the makeshift family that had formed around the restaurant.

On the eighth day, Juniper shook her head at the offer of curried carrot and kumara soup finished with pea shoots, cilantro, and a vibrant basil oil. "It sounds delicious, but I couldn't."

"Why not, dear?"

"Because then I'll need to tell you something about myself, but I want it to be the other way around today. Won't you tell me about yourself, Mabel? About your family? Do you have children and grandchildren?"

Mabel plastered a bright smile onto her face. "I'm afraid not, dear. It's just me. Now, let me get you some soup."

"I'm sorry," Juniper murmured, flushing. "I've overstepped."

Mabel shook her head, still smiling brightly. "Not at all. It was thoughtful of you to ask." She brought Juniper a bowl, then moved away, tending to the tables of regular guests. Their warm, familiar company washed away her initial reaction, and by the time she got back to Juniper, she was ready to be more honest. "I always wanted children. It just never happened like that for me. But when I feed my regulars, I feel as if I'm at least their auntie or grandma."

"That's beautiful," Juniper said quietly, then offered her a tentative smile. "Still, I shouldn't have asked."

"Don't give it another thought, dear. Are you enjoying your soup?"

The next day, Juniper marched in with more determination than Mabel had seen from her before. She took her now-usual seat and announced, "I'll make it up to you."

Mabel blinked at the young woman as she set a bowl of beetroot and coffee soup topped with arugula, chives, borage, and calendula in front of her. "What do you mean?"

"It wasn't fair for me to ask for more than I've given. So here we go." Juniper took a deep breath and released it slowly. "My mom died when I was born. She was named Juniper, too. My dad named me after her, but I think it was too hard for him to call me by her name, so he called me Juny instead." She gazed into her bowl. "It's funny to hear that name again, even out of my own mouth. No one has called me that in a decade."

Something about the woman before her —this grown woman whose sinewy strength showed even through her diffident posture— looked for all the world like a lost child. Mabel ached to comfort her but had never been one for touch; food had always been her means of expression. Nevertheless, she reached out, only to find herself awkwardly patting the younger woman's shoulder a little too hard.

Juniper instinctively flinched away from the touch. The two stared at each other, then Juniper gave Mabel a bit of a smile. "The soup is delicious, as always," she said.

"Are you scared of me, Juniper? Have I done something to make you uncomfortable?"

"What do you mean?"

"Ever since the first day you came in, you've seemed as if you aren't quite sure you belong here, or if you're allowed to be here."

Juniper let out a little laugh. "That's nothing to do with you. You'd think that growing up traveling and wandering would make someone comfortable anywhere, right? I've found it just makes me equally uncomfortable everywhere, like there's never been any such thing as home."

"That sounds awful, dear."

"It is and it isn't," Juniper said with a shrug. "There's something to be said for feeling equally not-home everywhere."

The next day, Juniper showed up before opening time. "I hope I'm not interrupting," she said. "I needed to talk to you in private."

"You're not interrupting, dear. Have a seat. I'm afraid the soup isn't quite ready yet, but what do you need?"

Juniper dug into a pocket in her flowing trousers, then pulled out her hand in a tight, white-knuckled fist, as if she was afraid to drop something infinitely precious. "Hold out your hands," she murmured.

Mabel did as she was told, cupping her outstretched hands as Juniper carefully handed over what she had been holding: twenty or thirty small, shriveled balls in varying shades of brown with a hint of purplish blue opacity. "What are these?" Mabel asked.

"Smell them," Juniper urged.

Mabel brought her hands to her face and sniffed: a hint of spice and some woodsiness like the sap of a freshly broken pine branch. She rubbed one of the spheres to release more fragrance, and a bright, sweet note added its voice to the aromatic choir. She had never smelled anything quite like it. "Is this…?" she asked, not daring to finish the sentence.

"Juniper."

"How did you get these?"

Juniper gave a diffident shrug, though her face spoke to an internal struggle against showing too much emotion. "I explored. That's what I do."

"You went exploring out there in the wilds?"

"I don't hurt them," Juniper said, her face suddenly hard and her shoulders tensing. "I got all the clearances, I don't light fires, I don't take more than I need."

"I'm sure you do it all very well, dear. I wasn't questioning that, only it seems terribly lonely and dangerous out there all by yourself. Is there some nice young person who keeps you company?"

Juniper's defensive posture vanished, and she laughed softly. "You're very kind to worry. No, it's just me. I grew up exploring with my dad, and he taught me to take care of myself. Anyway, I was exploring, and I found a juniper tree. I think it's the last one. I didn't dare take too many berries." Her eyes took on the faraway look that Mabel was beginning to find all too familiar.

"Naturally you took them to scientists and restorationists to try to bring the species back?"

"Of course, that's the first thing I did," Juniper said.

"Of course," Mabel acknowledged quietly.

"They took most of them, tested them, and said they weren't viable. I guess the tree I found was a female, and there aren't any males left to pollinate her."

"Couldn't they do something with cloning or cross-fertilization?" Mabel wasn't really quite sure of how anything to do with cloning or cross-fertilization worked, but she had chatted over bowls of soup with enough people over the years to have heard that both methods had been successful in bringing species back.

"Yes. Actually, the species restorationists I talked to said it should be relatively easy."

"That's wonderful, dear! You've found a way to bring back your namesake."

"Not exactly." Juniper stared out the window, evidently lost in her thoughts.

Mabel waited patiently, the precious berries still cupped in her hands. After some time, she said, "Here, dear, you ought to have these back."

Juniper offered her a wan smile. "They're for you."

"For me?"

"Yes." Juniper let out a sigh. "That's why I'm here. See, it should be possible to bring the species back from the brink, now that we know one is alive. The fact that it's female makes it even easier, because we have the berries. The problem is that there are so many equally worthy projects, and only so much time and resources."

"The restorationists don't want to work on this one?"

"Oh, I'm sure they want to! My dad wanted to restore every species he could, and I know it broke his heart every time he had to say 'no' to a project. But that region's ecosystem has been thriving without juniper this far, so it's not a vital missing link in nature. And nobody in hundreds of years has tasted its berries, so it's not considered to be, as they put it, 'of major practical or cultural significance' to people, either. That means it'll go to the end of the list, and by the time they get to it in years or decades, that last tree might be gone."

Mabel was finally beginning to understand. "You want me to cook with these."

Juniper nodded. "I've spent most of my life traveling the wilds. For the last few months, I've been traveling the cities instead, looking for someone who makes magic with food."

"Why?"

"So I can meet with the people in charge of the culinary branch of the restoration council and convince them to change their minds."

⁂

Mabel strategized carefully. She would save as many berries as possible for Juniper's meeting, but she needed to learn how they worked. She had some sense of the berries' flavor from their aroma, but the only way to really know how to cook with them was to experiment.

That wasn't to say Mabel would be reckless. She had a plan. First, she wrapped a few of the berries in a piece of thin kitchen cloth, tying it off into a little bundle. That way, she'd be able to cook it in the broth but easily find it afterward to reuse the contents if possible. She crushed a few more berries in her mortar and pestle.

Now came the hard part: trying to pair ingredients with something she had never cooked with before. The berries' aroma reminded her a bit of bay leaves, so she began with that as her inspiration, creating a stock from roasted carrots and charred onions before adding potatoes and apples. The little sachet of juniper went in as the soup simmered away. After an hour, she pulled out the sachet and puréed the small portion of simple soup, served it into two little bowls, and sprinkled the crushed berries on top.

Juniper arrived just on time.

Kai Holmwood

"Are you ready?" Mabel asked. "It's not much, certainly not worthy of being the first time a human has eaten these berries in hundreds of years, but it will help me understand how to cook with them."

Juniper nodded silently.

Simultaneously, the two women picked up their spoons and took their first bites. Juniper's face was downturned, hiding any expression, but Mabel was her own harshest critic anyway. "Well, that didn't work at all," she said.

At that, Juniper looked up at her. "It's quite nice."

"It's fine. It isn't remarkable. The juniper is sharp and bright, and the other ingredients are too gentle to support its flavor."

Juniper took another bite, her brow furrowed in concentration. "I see what you mean now that you describe it that way."

"Tomorrow, I'll do it better," Mabel promised.

The next day, Mabel made a tomato-based soup with white beans, toasted garlic chips, rosemary, and roasted bell peppers. "The theory," she said, "is that the acidity of the tomato and the bite of the garlic are bold enough to stand up to and support the sharpness of the juniper. The beans provide substance without being overwhelmingly flavorful on their own. The rosemary is there to bring out the herbaceous notes in the juniper, and the bell peppers give just a bit of sweetness so the whole thing isn't too harsh."

"It sounds almost as good as it smells," Juniper said with a hint of a grin.

They ate again. And again, Mabel was dissatisfied. "I went too far the other way," she bemoaned. "Now the juniper doesn't stand out enough to impress anyone."

To Mabel's surprise, Juniper didn't look disappointed at all. Instead, her smile was unusually warm as she said, "Then you know everything you need to know to find the perfect middle ground."

"I hope so," Mabel said. "After all, next time is my last chance."

Three days later, Mabel began cooking before dawn. First, she caramelized onions so slowly that they were almost formless by the time they were sweet and brown. She roasted parsnips, fennel root, and cabbage. She ground caraway seeds into the finest powder. All of those went into a pot together with a few juniper berries and a simple broth to simmer. Once everything was soft, she puréed the mixture, then poured it through a sieve to ensure perfect smoothness before returning the pot to the heat. As the soup cooked, she sautéed chanterelles and tossed them with thyme. Finally, she crushed the last few juniper berries as finely as she could.

FOUR PEOPLE HAVE ARRIVED. WELCOME, JUNIPER, ANTON, CARYS, AND SOL.

Mabel walked out into the dining area, wiping her hands on her apron. "Welcome," she said. "Please have a seat wherever you'd like, and I'll bring your soup out for you momentarily." She did her best to keep her composure, but the anxious look on Juniper's face made that almost impossible.

Mabel ladled the soup into four bowls, but brought them to the table two at a time; she didn't dare take any chances. Once she had set the bowls down, she drizzled each with a few drops of black garlic oil, scattered the chanterelles on top, then carefully —oh, so carefully— sprinkled the last crushed juniper berries onto each portion. And then she excused herself, went into the back room, and waited.

An eternity later, she heard the front door close, then a single set of footsteps coming toward the kitchen.

"Mabel?"

Mabel pushed herself up from the seat and rushed out. "How did it go?" she asked. "Did they like it? Did *you* like it? Was the juniper prominent enough? Did they say anything?" As the questions tumbled out, she looked Juniper up and down. The younger woman's entire body was trembling, and her eyes were reddening with unshed tears.

Silently, Juniper bit her lower lip and nodded. "They loved it," she whispered, then the words spilled out in a flood to match Mabel's. "Oh, Mabel, they loved it! They ate every bite. They said they hadn't realized how remarkable it would be, or that it would taste so different from the herbs and spices we already use. And— and they said they would push to research it *this* year. They even asked me to stay in Oakstead so I can learn about the process. It's not quite a guarantee, but— oh, it's the closest thing to one! It's really going to happen."

"You did it, Juny," Mabel said, pulling the young woman into a warm embrace. She felt the younger woman's frame winning the fight against sobs, but she also felt a wet warmth on her shoulder that meant that tears, at least, had snuck through Juniper's defenses. They stayed like that until, with one shuddering breath, the tension went out of Juniper's body.

Juniper pulled back and gazed into Mabel's face, not bothering to wipe away the salty wetness on her cheeks. "*We* did it. I'm so, so sorry you even didn't get to try any," she said, looking ready to start crying anew.

"As soon as there are enough berries, we'll make a batch big enough to feed everyone in Oakstead," Mabel promised.

"Of the same soup? You never make the same soup twice!" Juniper was laughing now, even as tears still glistened in her eyes.

"I'll make an exception just this once. Now, are you ready?" Mabel asked.

"For what?"

"To come home with me, Juny. You'll need a place to live if you're going to stay around for a while."

Juniper's eyes searched her face for what felt like a long time. Mabel hardly dared to breathe, in case something she did pushed the young woman away. Finally, Juniper gave her the most brilliant smile she had ever seen. "I'd like that," Juniper said. "I'd like to have a home."

COUNT IT AN ANCHOR
BY TAFFY LAMBA

Love. That's a weird thing, right?

I've heard a man claim it's the strongest magic, capable of curing all ills. Of course, he was trying to sell me his patented love potion at the time, but it's an interesting pitch. People profess their love everywhere: in their homes and crowded streets, to their partners, to the stars, even to that almost burnt pizza crust that tastes better than the whole pie. People love everything, including love itself.

Love makes you do things you normally would never consider. For example, going out into the town center in the middle of rush hour even though you hate crowds. However, that's not my plight. It's Lana's. I couldn't go into town because we don't want me causing another citywide incident. So, even though I should be the one trekking across the city, it's my best friend and roommate doing it instead. Just one of the bizarre ways love works.

Unfortunately, I can't really say I feel love. Not recently. I'm having a tough time feeling anything, to be fair, but love stands out. Because when you love something, it brings you joy. You look forward to it. Yet nowadays the only thing I look forward to is returning to the pit of darkness that is sleep. And gosh, I would kill for more sleep. After all, no one's here to stop me. Lana is still in town and who really knows when or if she'll be back? What would she do if I went to sleep right now? Nothing. She's powerless to stop me. Still, I don't head upstairs where I know the temptation will overwhelm me. Instead, I pull up a dining chair to the window, watching the outside world.

The city outside our tiny flat is bright and loud. The bitter heat of yesterday has dissolved into a cool, breezy afternoon, the wind taking leaves up in flight. The people walking the street have gone to take advantage of the weather, encouraging me to do the same. Therefore, I rise out of my chair and lock the front door. It's all for show, I know, but it makes me feel better, calmer. It takes the edge off the magic buzzing restlessly underneath my skin.

Resuming my seat at the window, I watch the people outside go about their day. A woman is spewing Latin curses at her son who looks like he'll burn down the whole block if that flush on his cheeks is anything to go by. Demons are terrible at the whole parenting thing. They rarely get the opportunity, and no one is eager to help them. Although, I guess it should be common knowledge that you don't command your child to return to the eighth circle of hell unless you want him to throw a tantrum. And look at that tantrum. His hair is on end now and there's a flame flickering in each hand.

I really should go get the ward. Lana and I do not have demon spawn covered in our insurance. We have demon, not demon spawn, and that's where they get you. I have had three people tell me that Loy Insurance refused to cover them. I mean, I don't trust Loy— their marketing division is headed by a genie. It's a scam if ever I saw one. Still, better them than CHIWa. I'd rather lose my money than my soul, honestly.

Why am I thinking of CHIWa? Dang it, the kid.

I barely have enough time to duck before a fireball comes hurtling to the window. The glass shatters against the inferno. Flames lick at my face before being sucked away harmlessly into the small stone hippo sitting on the windowsill. Its eyes shine briefly before dimming and the stone reverts back to wool, leaving a knitted doll in its place. As the window repairs itself, I breathe a sigh of relief, grateful to Lana for putting up the ward.

The demon lady and her child have left by the time the soot is swept away but I don't mind. You can't really scold a kid for acting on his nature and anyway, his mother would probably yell about how witches are disrespectful. Luckily, Lana putting up the ward has left me feeling inspired.

I plop myself into the rocking chair, picking up my knitting needles and some pink wool. Two more pairs of needles rise at the call of my magic. And thank Jupiter the magic is still working. Three days without my antidepressants is pushing it, but thankfully we're still functioning. Together, we start clack-clack-clacking our way towards a new defense ward. Maybe a porcelain elephant this time. Perhaps one with ears that can hear what Mr Lungu from next door says about us.

Unsurprisingly, it isn't long before a sigh emanates from deep within my bones, sapping me of all resolve. And I say 'unsurprisingly' because did I really expect the motivation to last? When was the last time I felt inspired to do anything constructive? I couldn't even muster the energy for breakfast this morning; first fail of the day. First of many, apparently.

Frustrated, I toss the needles away, having only knitted two rows. They're uneven and crummy, so it was a waste to begin with. Wards need careful stitching, not necessarily perfect as everyone thinks, just even enough to tell the magic that you care about your work. These lines are abysmal. I hold them in my hands and they unravel. Upset, I will them back into a tight ball but the wool protests, buzzing angrily until it bursts into lines of barbed wire.

Blood drips onto the floor and I panic. The drop is too sudden. If Lana doesn't come back soon, my magic might fail, and we'll get a repeat of last June. I'd rather not be trapped here for another week.

Casting a spell to heal my hands, I pick up my phone and type out a message. Feeling like an idiot, I promptly delete it. Lana knows I need my pills. How could she not? I've been badgering her about them for days even though it's not her fault the chemist ran out last week. She's doing more than I deserve by going out to get them for me. She doesn't need me bothering her every second. Gosh, I must be so annoying.

A chill runs through me as the temperature drops a few degrees.

"Fine," I say. "I'm not annoying. I'm just..."

But what's the point? Saying I'm not annoying doesn't change the fact that I am. I should accept it. I'm annoying, I'm selfish, and I spam her phone while she's doing me a favor. I'd hate to have me for a roommate.

The room drops colder.

In the kitchen I hear the houseplants wailing, complaining about the chill. I'd love to help, really. It's just, I don't think I give a crap anymore. Sure, they might hate me, but who doesn't right? The universe itself doesn't seem too fond of me, if it let the pharmacy run out of medicine I need to be a functional human witch. Hell, even my magic must hate me. We've been together all my life— it should know I hate the cold. But who cares about Rey? Let's punish her for being ill with the thing she hates the most. Let's make her feel worse.

I want to sleep. I'm tired. I'm done. I don't care what Lana says because she doesn't understand that I need to rest.

Heaving, I trudge up the stairs, headed for my room. The steps groan under my weight and sway, trying to tip me over. The walls snap, tearing up the wallpaper. Jagged wood planks jut out threateningly, the shredded wallpaper now covered by frost. The whole house shudders when I breathe. Everything is exhausting.

I make it to the landing upstairs and notice a portal outside my door. It glows purple and from it peeks the head of a goblin, two, three. Soon, a whole tribe is falling through the portal. They stare at me for a moment, obviously wondering why they would be summoned —goblins are a nuisance and they know it— before barrelling downstairs. Kitchen pots and pans ring out as they ransack the house.

I climb onto the bathroom sink, uncomfortable thanks to the taps digging into my back, and project my consciousness downstairs. My magic nearly splits my mind with the effort, but thankfully it's an old trick that I've perfected over the years.

Lana's face is a mask of horror. Looking around, I understand the concern. The living room is covered in ice and shrouded in darkness. Deadly icicles poke through the walls and various portals litter the space, all glowing brilliantly, uncontrolled. My needles have managed to craft a pair of handcuffs and a straitjacket, and now they're working on unravelling the curtains.

Lana shuts her eyes and breathes, eyes crinkling with the strain. As one, the portals collapse on themselves, but my magic retaliates, firing a jolt of energy at her. I feel it from my perch on the bathroom sink, the magic lashing out, vengeful.

With a gasp, Lana teleports into the kitchen, looking around at the damage. The goblins have torn the backdoor off its hinges and escaped, leaving ruins in their wake. Cabinets have their doors ripped off, dishes lie on the floor in piles of broken ceramic. The electrical wires exposed in the walls are a sparking fire hazard. What calls Lana's attention, however, are the houseplants, dry and brittle on the windowsill. She cradles the leaves, cooing sadly.

"I'm sorry," I offer, causing her to jump three feet.

"Where are you?" she gasps.

"Here."

"I mean where's your body?"

"Upstairs," I say.

She groans. "Rey, I told you not to go to sleep."

"I didn't," I scoff, suddenly petulant as she runs to the staircase. "I went to take a bath. And anyway, why shouldn't I go to sleep? You know I feel terrible."

"Which is why you shouldn't. Your magic is unstable when you're like this. I'll never get to you. Now stay awake, please."

I roll my metaphysical eyes. Of course, I know my magic is unstable; that's its defining trait at this point. But Lana's acting as if I'm a child.

I jolt as my body reacts to danger. Which reminds me—

"Don't go upstairs," I say to her. She's already halfway up, even as the stairs try to throw her off. Still, she can always turn back. In fact, she should turn back right now.

"You need your meds," she huffs.

See, this is what I don't get. How come she can tell me what to do but I can't? Not going to sleep is for my own good but she's allowed to dismiss my concern?

Lana makes it up the stairs finally and yanks my bedroom door open. She's already in the room before she realizes I'm not there.

"You're not asleep."

"I told you I came to take a bath," I snap.

"Oh. I'm proud of you," she says.

"Congratulations. Anyway…"

Using my magic, I shut the door just as she reaches it. It's for her own good, unless she wants to come face to face with whatever monster is at the door.

But hopefully the plants are okay. They scare easily.

Going to sleep is out of the question, so says the active portal. Although, I could always try to teleport through it, if I want to risk falling into the Realm of the Nyau, that is. It's not worth it.

Instead, I head for the bathroom on the opposite end of the landing. I need a bath anyway. I started needing one days ago, in fact. I just didn't have the strength. But as I run the bath, I think I might.

I'm about to take off my shirt when something crashes at the door. The room vibrates violently as another crash sounds out.

"Stupid," I berate myself. I forgot to shut down the portal and now there's something nasty at the bathroom door and the only thing keeping it out is the ward Lana put there.

Speaking of Lana…

She's calling out for me. So maybe if I'd just stayed downstairs for a few more minutes… so stupid.

Taffy Lamba

She pounds her fist on the wood once before teleporting herself out of the room and onto the landing. She's a lot better than I am at teleportation, and she's not all that great so what does that say about me?

"Don't do that," she shivers. "I can feel it getting colder, don't you dare put yourself down. You have great qualities." Oh, here we go. "My wards are only effective because you make the best conduits out of anyone I know. Your knitting is amazing."

Couldn't even knit two rows today though.

Her lips turn blue as frozen stalagmites rip through the floorboards. Still, she pushes forward. It's impressive, really, how she perseveres amid all the hardship, only freezing when she crosses the landing.

"Rey," she calls, and the tremor in her voice has nothing to do with the cold. "Rey, there's a Nyau."

"Is that what that was?" Ancient Spirits of the dead come to beat the crap out of me and escort my soul to the afterlife.

"Don't be a jerk Rey, get rid of it."

"I didn't bring it."

"Your portals did."

"It was an accident."

"This is serious. If it sees me, it'll come after me."

"Do we even know if the legends are true? For all we know, it could be harmless."

"I don't want to find out!" she shrieks.

"I don't think it's seen you yet. You can still run."

"I'm trying to help you," she says, conjuring a fan to hide her face when the Nyau glances her way.

"I'm trying to help you too." I say as it takes a step towards her, forcing her to take one back.

"You know what," she says, backing away. "I can't do this. Your pills are downstairs." With that, she takes off running.

I guess that finally did it.

I could follow her, see where she goes, but I'm not in the mood to see someone I love leave my life for good because of something I did, even if I didn't mean it. They always say I shouldn't blame myself. *It's not my fault*, they argue, *I can't control it*. But I don't see anyone else here.

I return to my body, bones heavier than lead. The emptiness in my chest culminates in a deep sigh that never escapes, just sits there, pulling me under its weight.

I flee from it, crawling into the deepest recesses of my mind, and reach out for the darkness, the numbness. Sadly, it never comes. I can still feel how muted the world has become, still see my magic rend the walls. I want to scream, but the sound will be swallowed up by the unforgiving universe. Nothing exists. Not me, not Lana, not our flat. And the absence of everything hurts more than any wound.

The water overflows the bathtub, falling to the floor with an almost-sound. The room blurs, colors draining into muted greys. Is this what my mind looks like? Drab and dreary and grey? No wonder my magic is such a disappointment. It's cold and bleak, as I am.

The Nyau claws at the door, seeking entry, seeking to take me. But nothing it could do can compare to the damage my own mind inflicts.

Still, I don't want it to come in. But I don't fortify the ward either. I just hope it goes away.

The scratching grows louder, water soaks the floor, and the tears fall. I should feel something. Fear, perhaps, because an Ancient threatens to take my soul; concern for the wooden floorboards that are susceptible to rot; disgust, absolute disgust because I haven't showered in two weeks and everyone says I'm vile for it. Gosh, I should care that I drove away the one person who came back to me even when my magic was manifesting her greatest fears.

I want to be sad. Although I don't deserve it, really. Because sadness would mean feeling something that isn't the emptiness. And I deserve to be empty.

How did this even happen? I was fine last week. I can't recall the feeling, but I know I was happy. I know I looked forward to watching Mighty Magiswords even though Lana said it was silly. I know my baby blanket was so soft it made me giggle, and I know I loved the pepperoni pizza from Luyando's. Where did all that go?

My head hurts, pressure mounting as the hopelessness builds, until it explodes, shattering the windows and breaking down the door. I struggle to breathe as a new portal opens, this one a vortex above me, sucking everything into the ceiling. The Nyau at the door is pulled in, screeching an old language as it is swept up. I meet its eyes momentarily and my essence shakes within me. Fortunately, it is swallowed up quickly.

Unfortunately, I'm about to meet it again. As shards of glass fly through the room, I find myself present enough to shield my face, but not enough to grab hold of something. I'm pulled up into the air, snagging on something just as I'm about to disappear through the vortex.

Finally, after what has felt like centuries, my heart beats as I realize I have an anchor. Something keeping me tethered to the flat.

Splinters of glass graze my face, the water from the bath drenches me. All the chaos threatens to distract and pull me in, but I manage to focus, summoning just enough energy to teleport myself downstairs, where my anchor calls to me.

The fall to the kitchen floor is a painful one. But I made it, so that's a win.

The kitchen is bright, colors solid and plants green again, but already I can see everything greying at the edges, my magic draining the world. Lana sits at the kitchen table, drinking a cup of tea, her magic dancing all around the room and tidying up my mess. There's barely enough time for the shock to register because on the table sits a plastic container and I rush for it, the anchor pulling me along. I clutch the pill bottle in my hands desperately, choking out a sob. I just want to feel again and they're here. And maybe I'm a screw up, but I can finally feel like a screw up and not like I'm watching from the side-lines as a stranger lives my life.

A glass of water floats up to me and I grab it, taking down two pills. Tears flow unchecked, and my body crumples. Heaving sobs rack through me. The light is too bright, the floor too hard, the weather too calm. Everything overwhelms me. So, I hold my anchor close, folding myself around it. It presses painfully into my chest but all that matters is that it's here.

I wake up aching but feeling myself come back to the forefront of my mind. I'm in my bed. It's soft and the blanket smells of fabric softener. My room is bleak, but is regaining some color, mostly blue and white. Also, my head hurts. It's been hurting for a while, now that I think of it. Did I just get used to that? I should get that checked. Most importantly, however, my magic finally feels settled within my bones. It is no longer the itching, foreign thing of the past few days.

Despite the throb in my skull, I get out of bed and begin my descent to the kitchen. The landing is a maze of icy daggers. I wave a hand and they melt away, leaving a mess of puddles behind. I'll have to come back and clean it up once I feel better.

Padding down the stairs, I try to fix as much damage as I can. The shredded wallpaper knits itself back together under my touch, but the wall remains torn apart. The floor is still freezing under my bare feet but at least it's stopped moaning. The living room is flooded and covered with tangled thread. The needles are still.

I make it to the kitchen and try not to be surprised. Lana is there, talking to one of the plants. When it spots me, it turns away with a huff.

"You'll have to make it up to them," Lana says, facing me.

"I'll bet." I move to touch one of the leaves and suddenly the succulent becomes a thorny bramble.

Lana grimaces. "You really have to make it up to them."

"Yeah," I say around the finger in my mouth. The tang of blood makes me want to gag, and the look of pity Lana levels me makes my face heat in shame. "I thought you left."

"I wouldn't just leave you," she frowns.

And I feel stupid because I always do this, and she always says she'll be there for me forever. It's just...

"I feel insecure sometimes," I mumble.

"Oh, I know," she laughs. "But I need you to trust me enough to know I won't just abandon you. Like you would never abandon me."

"Thank you," I say. "And I'm sorry." She smiles a small smile, and I just hope my apology is enough.

I've been trying, I still am. And days like this? Days when everything goes wrong happen occasionally because I'm a— okay, maybe I'm not necessarily a screw up. But days like this do occur.

"Maybe it's fate," I sigh, taking a seat. "Maybe it's fate that disasters like this happen."

She blinks at me, unimpressed. "You said that about our names."

"No but listen, I already know a Delphin from high school. It can work."

She rolls her eyes but smiles anyway. "I don't think it's fate for you to have bad days, Rey. We all have them. But you made it. And look at you, teleporting and everything. You're getting better at it."

"Yeah, well there was literally a vortex pulling me to death, of course I was able—" The look she levels me has me backtracking. "I mean, sure, I guess I'm getting better."

The resulting smile is blinding, it's pointless to resist smiling back.

"Please clean up this mess when you can," Lana says. "Your magic is touchy, and I don't want to call Loy. Oh, and I need a new ward for luck. Could you make me a dreamcatcher?"

"You want me to knit a dreamcatcher?"

"Yeah," she says. "You've got magic needles."

"And you have magic knives, you don't see me asking for an enchanted cake."

"I literally ran across town for you today. Nearly got run over."

"Really? I did all your laundry two weeks ago."

"I didn't know we were counting that."

"I didn't know we were counting my *mental well-being*, Lana."

"Fine," she grumbles, crossing her arms. "But you will make me a dreamcatcher, right?"

"I'll make a nice blue one," I smile. And then she smiles. And I love that smile. And I love her. And our little home and the childlike plants in the windows and the Mighty Magiswords. Hell, I could even say I love my magic. It's odd how that works, isn't it? Because love is weird. Weirder still when you can finally feel it. ♀

Taffy Lamba

ANOTHER DAY ON THE

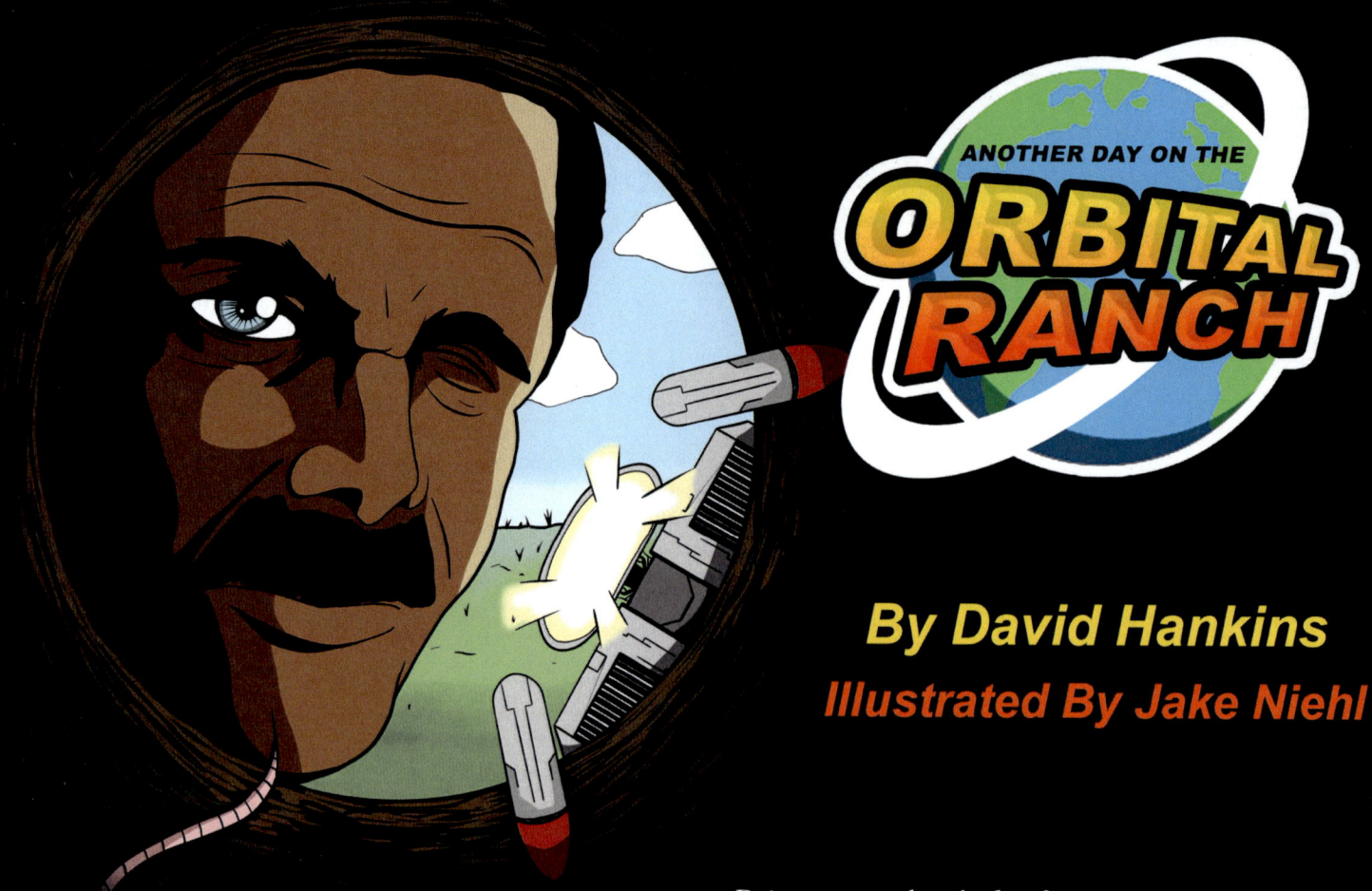

ORBITAL RANCH

By David Hankins
Illustrated By Jake Niehl

Sunshine beamed through Skyfield Ranch's hexagon-paned dome, warming Paul's neck as he crouched inside an in-ground plumbing junction. Green fields spread to the orbital ranch's artificial horizon, broken only by scattered outbuildings and the ranch house in the distance. Dairy cows chewed their cuds and watched Paul curiously. He ignored them and cranked his plumber's wrench, struggling to loosen a clogged pipe.

It felt good to work with his hands again. To have something he could control. Paul hated being Skyfield's Ops Chief; hated the million details that overwhelmed him every day. But Gladys Skyfield expected her second husband to be just as competent as her first. Paul loved Gladys, but the expectations to fill a dead man's shoes were...exhausting. That's why he'd snuck out here. During these few peaceful moments doing his old job, life felt like just another day on the orbital ranch.

Paul grunted with effort and the six-inch pipe joint released with a squeal of abused metal. The joint clanged down at Paul's feet. Brown sludge dribbled out with the fetid stench of liquefied manure. Skyfield Ranch boasted the latest in sustainable energy and the most powerful gravity generator in existence, but humanity still hadn't figured out how to handle crap without good old-fashioned plumbing.

Dairy cows produced a *lot* of crap.

Skitter, Paul's spider-drone pipe crawler, made a *tsk* sound from atop the pipe as it loosened. "Took you long enough."

Paul cocked an eyebrow and held out the wrench. "If you want to do the heavy lifting, be my guest."

Skitter rotated his flat head in the semblance of a head-shake. "Nah, just saying you're out of practice. It hasn't been the same since you moved into the big house. The other plumbers treat me like just another tool." Skitter kicked with his steel toed, rubber-treaded foot, producing a hollow echo from the pipe.

Paul grimaced. "Yeah, sorry about that." AI rights were a touchy subject these days. AIs had enabled humanity's shift into sustainable arcology and orbital farming, but they still weren't seen as individuals. Just smart tools.

Paul tapped the pipe. "Well, I'm here now. Shall we see what's clogged this thing?"

"Righto, boss-man." A tiny yet powerful light snapped on below Skitter's single optical input and he crawled over the pipe's edge and disappeared inside. Paul retrieved his tablet to watch Skitter's video feed and leaned back against pipes that disappeared into tight tunnels to both sides.

The clogged pipe before him rumbled with the rapid *thump-thump-thump* of rubberized feet on steel. Skitter gave a long whistle. "Found it!"

Paul eyed the video feed, brows scrunched. "What is that? A giant hairball?"

"You been throwing your glorious locks down the drain again?"

"Ha, ha," Paul said, deadpan, and ran fingers through his decidedly thinning hair. "See if you can break it up."

Skitter activated his sonic disruptor which made Paul's inner ear bubble. An articulated leg poked at the sludgy mass of hair, hay, and cow manure.

The clog rippled and moved, revealing beady red eyes and a long snout. Narrow teeth snapped at Skitter, and Paul jumped. He dropped the tablet and it slid under the pipe, just out of reach.

"That's a rat!" Paul yelled.

"What? Can't be," Skitter's voice echoed back. "Skyfield's rat population was exterminated fifty years— hey let go! That's my leg!" The pipe rattled and jumped. Screeches and thumps sent Paul scrambling for the tablet. He squatted in front of the pipe, straining to reach around it.

Skitter and the rat shot from the pipe, riding a wave of liquefied manure, and slammed into Paul's gut, driving the air from his lungs. He gasped, inhaled manure-filled air, and gagged. He didn't vomit, but it was a close thing.

The gush of released pressure died and Paul struggled *not* to draw deep breaths. He whipped around, looking for the rat. A *rat*? What the hell? Skitter's panicked voice drew his eyes to the right down the narrow pipe-filled tunnel.

"Go away! Go away! I. Am. Not. Your. Dinner! Ahhhhh..."

Skitter's light bounced inside the tunnel as he batted at the hissing rat. Then Skitter spun and bolted down the pipes, articulated legs flying, the rat waddling close behind him. The light dimmed with distance and the spider-drone's shrieks echoed then faded as he disappeared from view around a far corner.

Paul sat back with a squelch of liquid manure and swore. Loudly. He grabbed his tablet from a putrid puddle. Dead. He chucked it skyward, drawing concerned moos from his bovine audience.

Where in the *hell* had a rat come from? It couldn't be a survivor from the original infestation. Not after fifty years. It must have come in on...

Realization dawned and Paul swore again, but quietly and to himself. This was his fault. He'd switched feed suppliers last quarter to one with ridiculously low rates. Paul had wondered how AAA Feed Solutions made a profit while still paying Earth's expensive customs cleaning requirements.

Somehow, they'd bypassed customs. Paul had brought the rat in. Gladys was going to *kill* him!

🐀 🐀 🐀

Paul bounced on his four-wheeler's bench seat as he sped over sprawling fields toward the ranch house. The next nearest orbital ranch was just visible over Skyfield's western horizon. Urban sprawl had long since covered Earth's grasslands, but sustainable arcology let the megacities produce much of their own food. The balance —luxury items like milk and cheese— was produced by orbiting ranches like Skyfield where livestock had room to graze.

Paul bypassed the house's broad front porch and parked around back. The sprawling single-story building looked like a nineteenth-century farmhouse complete with faux-shingle siding and gingerbread trim. It served as both the Skyfield family home and the operations center for the ranch. Crew and ranch hands, all seventy-eight of them, lived below deck. A small cadre for such a massive station, but AI drones managed the majority of the workload.

Paul trudged into the Monitoring and Control Station. Stacked screens lined the MCS's walls with video and status displays. Two dark-skinned women sat kicked-back in their chairs, boots on desks. Sanvi, the middle-aged operator from India that Paul had expected to find, cocked an eyebrow at him and then wrinkled her nose. Yeah, he stank. Chloe, his eighteen-year-old stepdaughter whom he *hadn't* expected, glared from behind crimped curls. Chloe always glared at him. She thought Paul was a gold digger.

He wasn't, but convincing Chloe that he'd married her mother for love seemed beyond him. Paul had been flattered when Gladys had shown interest and fell hard during their brief courtship. Once he and Gladys started fighting, though, Chloe's disapproval had only grown.

Sanvi stopped his entry with a raised hand. "You ain't coming in here smelling like that, Ops Chief or no. What'd you do, bathe in sewage?"

"Um, sort of. Can you send a cleanup drone to the pipe junction in Pasture A3? My tablet died." Sanvi sat forward and tapped a screen as Paul added, "And I need a location on Skitter, my pipe-crawler."

Chloe's glare turned concerned and she dropped her boots to the floor with a thump. "What happened?"

Paul drew a deep breath. Every instinct told him to lie about the rat and the contaminated shipments, but bad news never aged well. Better that it came from him. "Skitter was chased away by a rat."

Sanvi's fingers froze over her control screen.

"By a *what*?"

"A rat. They headed eastward from the pipe junction."

Sanvi threw a schematic onto the screen by Paul's head. He craned around the doorway and saw Skitter's blinking icon. Sanvi leaned forward, eyes narrowed. "He's in Composting D."

"Thanks!" Paul turned to leave.

"Hold on," Sanvi said. "I'm sending Chloe with you."

"What?" he and Chloe said simultaneously.

"The cameras in Composting D are on the fritz. I sent the nearest cleaning drone in to assess, but he went offline too." Sanvi retrieved a small red satchel from a drawer and tossed it to Chloe. "Utility cameras and a control tablet. I want to see this rat." Chloe's lips pursed and she eyed Paul.

He smiled. "Happy to have you along."

Chloe clutched the bag and stomped out, careful not to touch Paul's soiled clothes. He turned a quizzical eye toward Sanvi. They'd been friends for years before he married the boss. What was she up to?

"You could have just given me the camera."

Sanvi rolled her eyes. "You and Chloe need to work out your issues. I love the girl, she's crazy smart, but I'm tired of her surliness whenever you're around. And Paul..."

His eyes narrowed at the warning tone.

"...I'm calling Gladys; something *you* should have done the second you knew we had rats."

"My tablet died!"

"And every four-wheeler has an emergency comm. No excuse. Rat infestations qualify as emergencies."

David Hankins

Paul clenched his jaw but nodded. She was right. Both as Ops Chief and as Gladys's husband, he should have called. He really wasn't looking forward to their next conversation.

Paul and Chloe sped down a dirt path under the crystalline dome, past grazing cattle and grass that waved gently in an artificial breeze. The four-wheeler's perpetual-motion engine purred quietly and Paul glanced at Chloe's tight expression. He fumbled for something to say. He hadn't expected joining a family to be quite so complicated.

"Nice day," he said, glancing upward.

"It's always a nice day here."

"Well, yeah, but sometimes it rains."

"On schedule."

Paul refrained from pursing his lips and let it drop. They passed through two automated gates between pastures before reaching a small outbuilding that provided elevator and stairwell access to the lower decks. They could have driven through the lower-deck corridors, but Paul liked feeling the sun and wind on his face. Plus, the smell of sunbaked fields almost overwhelmed his manure stench.

They dismounted and Chloe thumbed the elevator switch. The doors slid open with the antiseptic smell of a recent cleaning. "What brought you to the MCS?" he asked as they stepped inside. "I thought Gladys had you working herd management."

Chloe's face tightened. "Ranching is Mom's passion, not mine."

The elevator hissed downward and Paul considered what he knew about Chloe. She was tech-savvy. Liked working with the AI drones. "You were in MCS because Sanvi lets you tinker with the AIs, right?"

Her expression lightened a little. "Yeah, Sanvi's cool. And I don't tinker with the AIs. I talk to them. Just because they're manufactured, doesn't mean they're not people."

The elevator deposited them onto the first deck below field level. Paul chewed his lip as they turned left down a broad, low passageway. "Yet Skyfield's official position is against recognizing AI sentience. 'Utopia can't run itself,'" he said, quoting the late Tom Skyfield.

"What do you know?" Chloe's sudden fury made Paul flinch. "And why are you even interested? You're not my father. You're just the first pretty face Mom latched onto after Dad died." Chloe lengthened her stride and turned into Composting D.

Paul slowed, lips pursed. Great job mending fences. Not that he disagreed with Chloe's assessment. He'd never be the man Tom Skyfield had been but felt compelled to try. Yet after two rocky years, Paul worried that Gladys regretted her hasty re-marriage.

He followed Chloe into Composting D whose heavy air reeked of ammonia. The massive room was dimly lit and filled with ceiling-high steel bins and a dizzying array of pipes. Narrow aisles cut between the composting bins and ran along the walls.

Chloe pulled two sturdy minicams from the bag and clipped them to adjustable headbands. She thrust one at Paul and put on her own before retrieving a tablet. The screen flickered and she said, "Sanvi, are we connected?"

"Gotcha."

Through the tablet, Paul heard MCS's door slam and Gladys's sharp voice yelled, "Where's this rat?"

"We just connected," Sanvi said. "This is Paul's feed, that's Chloe's."

"Paul?" Gladys's tone turned hard. "If there's a rat *anywhere* in Skyfield Ranch, you and I are going to have a long talk about your cut-rate feed supplier."

Paul's jaw clenched. She'd reached the same conclusion he had. "Understood. Stand by." He drew a deep breath and motioned for Chloe to lead the way. She consulted the tablet's schematic and turned right toward Skitter's blinking icon. They turned left along the wall and passed a half-dozen steel composting bins.

Paul called out, "Hey Skitter, where you at, buddy?"

"Help me!" The spider-drone's terrified voice came from the back corner beyond the last composting bin.

They turned the corner and stopped dead. A roiling mass of brown and gray fur filled the narrow aisle. Rats atop rats. They hung from the compost bin's access ladder and looked down from pipes near the ceiling.

Every beady eye was fixed on Skitter. He swung slowly on a dangling light fixture in the center of the aisle like a trapeze artist performing for his adoring fans. Furry snouts followed his sway, illuminated by his slowly waving spotlight. Chloe stepped back, a hand over her mouth.

A shiver crawled down Paul's spine. "How you doing, Skitter?" he said softly.

"How does it look like I'm doing?" The spider-drone's spotlight snapped toward Paul, blinding him. "I'm about to become rat food!"

"I don't think rats eat drones. Not enough meat on your bones."

"Yeah? Tell that to Bobo over there." The spotlight swiveled and illuminated the remains of a wheeled cleaning drone. It leaned against the wall beyond the rat swarm, detached arms shredded and cybernetic innards scattered across the floor.

Paul's breath caught and he glanced at Chloe, brow furrowed in confusion.

She kept her voice low. "All station wiring is sheathed in a plastic alternative derived from peanuts. It's economically sustainable, but..."

Paul nodded. "But it's like catnip to rats." He narrowed his eyes at Bobo, then pointed. "Look at the bite marks on his framing. The rats were *gnawing* his aluminum."

Chloe swore darkly, making Paul's eyebrows raise. He glanced back again and she said, "Their teeth can cut metal. I'd heard rumors of mutated rats on other stations, of a new subspecies evolved to thrive in space, but I didn't believe them."

Paul grimaced. "And that's how they've stayed hidden. They chewed into sealed walls, nested, and bred." He eyed the writhing mass of rats. There were easily over a hundred. He did some quick math. "Rats reproduce exponentially. There could be hundreds in a few months. Thousands within a year."

Skitter's voice turned sarcastic. "Thank you for the biology lesson. Really fascinating. Now get me out of here!"

"Hold up!" Gladys's voice cut in. "You're not going anywhere, drone, not while you have the rats' undivided attention. Those vermin are a risk to this station. Paul, what's your extermination plan?"

He should have expected the question. Tom had always had a plan for everything. Paul was more focused on the problem in front of him. He needed to save Skitter. He scratched at his ear which had been bubbling since they'd arrived. His fingers paused as an idea hit him. "Skitter, turn off your sonic disruptor."

"Hell no! That's the only weapon I have against these monsters!"

"It's attracting them! You can't smell tasty enough to explain all of this." He waved at the enraptured horde.

One of the wires holding Skitter's swing abruptly dropped free, chewed through from above. Skitter's light swung in a pendulum arc toward the ladder and rats strained to reach him. The horde's chittering redoubled in volume.

Paul swore and backed into the corner, pushing Chloe aside. He eyed the distance to the spider-drone and to the horde's far side. "Turn it off, Skitter."

"But—"

"Now!"

Skitter whined but the bubbling in Paul's ear disappeared.

Rodent chitters paused and Paul sprang into a run. Three steps and he leapt over the rats.

"Gotcha!" he yelled, snatching Skitter. Paul misjudged his grip and caught the light fixture as well. They swung up toward the ceiling and Paul's eyes bulged at the rats just above him.

The wire snapped.

Paul barely had time to yell before they crashed onto the rats and his breath whooshed out. It was like landing on the lumpiest bed in the world. He sucked in a breath and rats squealed out from under him, clawing and biting. Paul scrambled to his feet, flinging rats off him. They scattered and Skitter clutched his arm like a rescued cat.

Gladys's voice was like a bullhorn through Chloe's tablet. "What the hell was that? Tom never would have risked the station to save a *drone*!"

"I'm not Tom!" Paul yelled, pent-up frustration suddenly pouring out. "I liked him, everyone did, but I'll never be Tom. I've got faults, but so did *he*, and his blindness toward AI sentience ranked at the top of the list. *I* won't sacrifice a drone, a *friend*, for anything. There's another way."

Resounding silence followed Paul's outburst. He glanced at Chloe's shocked expression then looked straight at her utility cam and spoke to Gladys. "Call the dock. Have them prep an empty shipping container —one that opens at both ends— as a trap. Skitter and I will lead the rats inside like the damned pied piper. Then we lock 'em in and ship 'em back where they came from."

Paul's heart thumped in his chest as Gladys's silence stretched. Finally, she said, "That'll work. They'll be ready in fifteen minutes."

Paul sagged in relief. The dock was a ten-minute walk from here. He eyed Skitter in his arms, realizing that he'd just volunteered his friend as rat bait.

The spider-drone shook his head. "You've got to be joking."

Paul smiled encouragingly. "Don't worry, buddy, I'll be with you the whole way. No other drones will die like Bobo did back there."

Skitter's optical sensor regarded him blankly. Drones weren't great at facial expressions. He gave an electronic sigh.

"Fine. Let's do this."

The rats were faster than Paul had expected. He and Skitter left Composting D at an easy jog, Skitter riding Paul's shoulder, singing his sonic tune while the rats poured from every nook and cranny.

A rat nipped at Paul's heels. He shrieked, jumped, and broke into a full run. Skitter bounced but kept all eight feet wrapped firmly around Paul's shoulder. They passed into the main corridor, a high-ceilinged roadway with two lanes.

To keep his mind off the ravening horde chasing them, Paul muttered, "I think Gladys is mad at me."

Skitter snorted, an amusing sound since he didn't have a nose. "You think? Why'd you even marry the old crone?"

"Hey, she's no older than I am."

"You make my point, baldy."

Paul chuckled, settling into the rhythm of running. "I married Gladys because, under that gruff exterior, she's surprisingly thoughtful and caring. You don't see it, not many do, but Gladys pours her heart and soul into running this ranch."

He glanced back and frowned. Chloe followed them, a safe distance behind the horde, but she didn't concern him. There were more rats than before. Lots more. "Anyway, sorry I roped you into this. I should have asked first."

"Humans don't ask AIs. You demand and program."

"Yeah, but we shouldn't. You're the beating heart of this ranch. Skyfield wouldn't exist without AIs." They passed an AI forklift hauling feed pallets. Its optical sensor eyed the strange procession but the fork continued on its programmed course.

Another forklift from a cross-corridor turned into Paul's path, then screeched to a halt. He jinked to the left, stumbled, but kept running. He glanced back again. The rat swarm parted around the machine like a hairy river. They were closer than before, the nearest just a yard behind him.

Paul burst into a sprint, breath coming fast. He rounded the corner into the dock and his eyes bulged.

The dock was in chaos. AI forklifts zipped past, frantically emptying a metal shipping container in the center of the expansive bay. Crew members screamed directions at drones. The burly dock foreman saw Paul and shouted at a backing forklift. The AI abruptly turned with squealing tires so it wouldn't run over Paul. Its load overbalanced and a barrel hit the deck with a *boom*. The lid popped off spewing thick brown sludge. Fortified Liquid Feed. FLF smelled like sweet oats but was slippery as oil.

Paul hit the FLF at a dead run. He couldn't stop. His feet slid out from under him and he splashed onto his belly with a yell. Skitter flew from his shoulder, landed beyond the spill, and rolled.

The rat horde didn't even pause. They swarmed over Paul, tiny claws and heavy bodies pushing him into the sludge. FLF pressed between his lips, oversweet and slimy.

Then they were gone.

David Hankins

Paul raised his head, gaze following the sludgy trail of tiny footprints to the container. The last rat disappeared inside and the foreman slammed the doors closed. Skitter was nowhere to be seen.

"Skitter!" Paul wiped his lips and scrambled, slipping and sliding out of the spill. His eyes flew to the container's back corner. He couldn't see the doors. Had Skitter made it through?

"Skitter! Skitter!"

He stumbled forward, boots slippery from the FLF.

Skitter's spidery form peered over the container's top edge. "Well, that was exciting."

Paul sagged in relief. "You're alive!"

"No thanks to you and your fancy footwork."

Paul chuckled, but his relief was short-lived. Gladys stormed toward him from an elevator. She was a more leathery version of Chloe: dark and lithe but with an air of unquestioned authority. Paul turned toward her, a dripping, smelly mess. Chloe appeared in the entrance he'd just slid through.

Paul forestalled Gladys's opening barrage with a raised hand. "Yes, the rats are my fault and we'll talk about that soon. First, we have a problem that only Chloe can fix."

Chloe pulled up short. "Me?"

"I need you to coordinate an AI-drone sweep of Skyfield Ranch. There's no way we found all the rats, but I'm not sending drones out alone to get swarmed. They trust you and *I* trust you to keep them safe as they search. You'll need comms, cameras, sonic disruptors…work the details with Sanvi in MCS."

He turned to the foreman who had leaned against the metal shipping container, thick arms crossed. "Prep more containers for traps and see if you can order a shuttle from our old supplier to deliver 'em to AAA Feed Solutions. AAA gave us the rats, they can deal with them. Oh, and file a customs complaint against AAA too, would you?"

The foreman grinned and threw a mock salute before turning away and barking orders. Paul drew a deep breath and faced Gladys.

Her glower faded, replaced by a curious expression. Her head cocked slightly to one side. "Good plan. I knew you had a knack for leadership. Thought I'd see it long before now."

The words should have stung, but Gladys was always blunt. Paul frowned. "I'm not a planner, I'm a plumber. Being the Ops Chief is all about seeing the big picture while managing a million little details every day. Tom was awesome at the job, but I'm not Tom. I've been swamped ever since I took over and this" —he waved at the container of rats— "is the result." Paul sighed and shoved his hands in his pockets. He grimaced as FLF oozed around his fingers. "Plumbing is about crisis management. Find the problem, fix the problem. That's all I'm doing."

Gladys nodded. "I came down here to fire you. You're a horrible Ops Chief."

Paul snorted. "Agreed."

"And I'm on the edge of divorcing you."

Paul's chest tightened, but he drew a deep breath. "Because I'm bad at job I never wanted? I thought you married me for my rugged charm and dashing good looks. Still got those." He smiled, but it felt weak.

"Those are nice, but not a reason to keep a man around." Gladys's expression remained stern, though her eyes were sad. Her shoulders slumped. "Something has to change, Paul. This" —she pointed between them— "isn't working."

Paul's smile dropped. "Then let me be me, not a shadow of Tom. We can cherish his memory, but let's make new memories of our own."

Gladys's gaze took in Paul's disheveled appearance then settled on his face. He felt in that moment that she finally saw him as *him*. She nodded. "That's fair, but you're still fired."

Paul's grin returned. "Thank God!"

Gladys eyed him, uncertainty in her eyes. "What'll you do now? As *you*?"

Paul's heart did a little flip. Was she asking about his next job, or about *them*? Should he walk away before she divorced him? Could he?

No. He'd never quit on anything in his life. "I think 'Maintenance Chief' would fit me better. I like fixing problems, and not just mechanical ones. I want to fix" —he waved a finger between them— "this."

A warm smile cracked Gladys's stern demeanor. "Me too." She drew a deep breath then let it out, her shoulders relaxing. "You're a good man, Paul. Stubborn, but honest. *That's* why I married you."

"*I'm* stubborn? Have you looked in the mirror recently?"

Gladys's smile turned into a smirk then she cocked an eyebrow at the mess around them. "Looks like you've got your work cut out for you, Maintenance Chief."

He nodded, unsurprised at the subject change. "Yup." Maintenance was largely automated, but that would give Paul a chance to work more closely with the AI drones. Speaking of which… "I'm going to go clean up. Can you meet me in the MCS? We need to talk about the AI drones and I want Chloe in that conversation. The AIs are integral to Skyfield Ranch and it's time we recognized that."

Gladys's eyes narrowed, but she nodded before turning back to the elevator. Paul drew a deep breath. That argument hadn't gone nearly as badly as he'd expected. There was hope yet.

Skitter had climbed off his perch and waited quietly to one side. Paul knelt and the spider-drone jumped onto his shoulder. He murmured into Paul's ear.

"Thanks. Not many people stand up for AIs."

Paul headed for the dock's decon shower. "Chloe said it best. AIs are people too. You deserve a chance to be whatever you want to be, not what we program you for."

Skitter seemed to consider this before he said, "So, Maintenance Chief. Let's talk upgrades. Have you heard about the new X7 processors? Well worth the cost. Oh, and I heard some forklift AIs complaining about overdue tread replacement. They need better traction. Speaking of treads, one of my feet came loose in the chase. Think you could…"

Paul smiled as Skitter's words rolled over him. He hadn't chosen an easy job, but it was one he understood. Soon the AIs would be able to choose as well.

Perhaps today wasn't just another day on the orbital ranch. It was a new day.

PETRICHOR
BY RICHARD A. SHURY

A standard day or month or year is dry wind across the plains, and not much else. It sits there, casing solid against the wind, sublayers absorbing the sun's immense heat and storing it in cells.

Once in a way, an animal will wander up, sniff at it and, bored, wander away again. Or a trail of ants will bump against it, usually going around and not across. There is even the occasional drop of bird poo, which gradually fades away.

Still, it waits, a tarnished boulder.

Once in a way, the Collector, large and slow, will dip down from the sky to collect the excess electricity. It can be heard from miles away, droning in and hovering. A cable dangles out of its belly to fit perfectly into a waiting port. The exchange is quick, and then the Collector is gone again, off to the next one. The port cover slides closed, and the machine is still once more.

It sits still, and waits.

Then there is a day, a day when the air changes, imperceptibly to anyone not local. But the natives, plant and nomad and steel alike, they look up and they sniff and they sense it. Days away still, but inevitable as the sunrise.

The first drops tink off its carcass, splashing against the hardened metal. When the downpour starts, when the rush really begins, when the flow rate exceeds a programmed value, it awakens. Or rather, it knows it is time to be awake; its legs uncoil, slowly, and it stands, a freak armadillo on metal feet. It walks slowly, always slowly. It tests the ground with slim appendages, sensors like antennae, sniffing for the scent of newly-wet soil. When it finds a suitably saturated area, it burrows in deep, churning the soil.

Within the machine, compartments slide open. Seeds and nutrients are prepared, mixed, dropped into chutes. Brought forth with gentle pressure, down flexible tubes, down at last into friendly ground. Deposited by the machine's tender arms, tucked into soil.

The machine moves on, to the next patch of ground. Over the scant days of rainfall it works tirelessly, diligently, planting and stirring the earth into life. And then, as quickly as they have come, the rains are gone again. The earth, tinged now with a thin green carpet, brushed once more by the sun's heavy heat. And every season, a little bit greener.

The machine retracts its legs, nestling into the waiting earth. It resumes its slumber. Inert but not dead. Just waiting. Simply waiting.

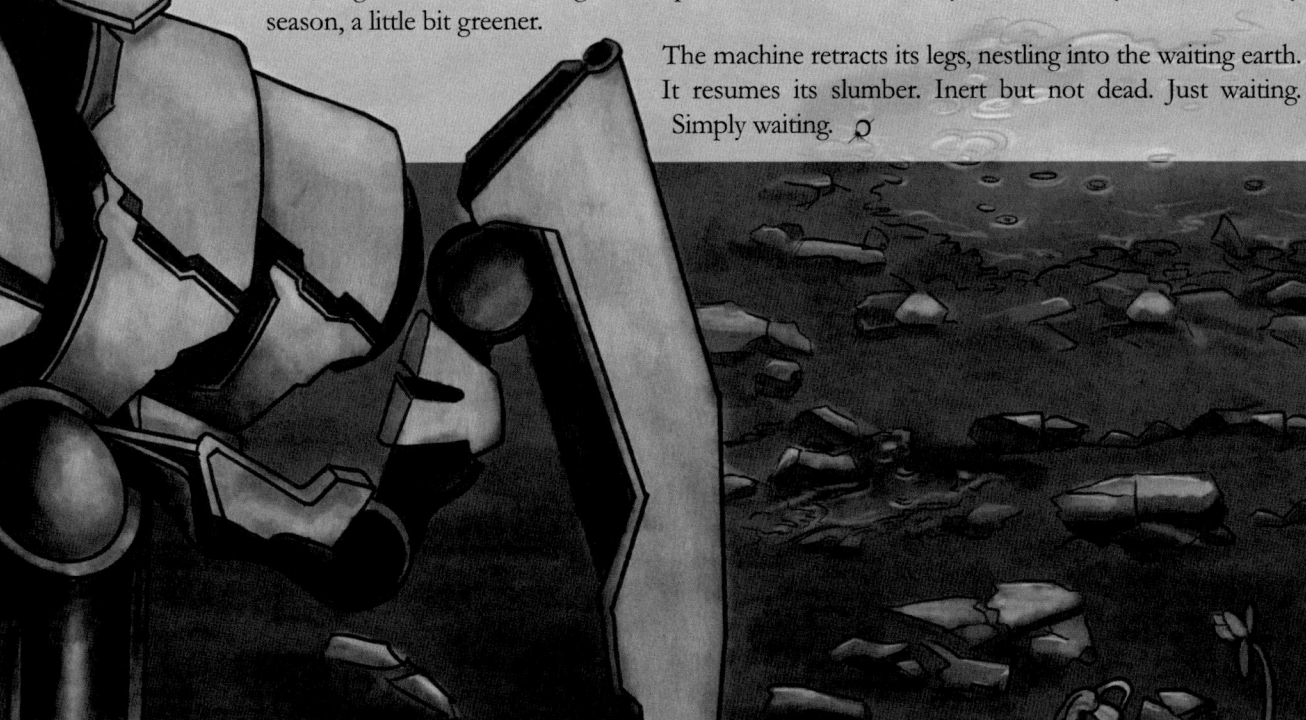

LIKE STARS DARING TO SHINE
BY SOMTO IHEZUE

When the boy opens his housing unit's steel door and the incandescent lights pour into his face, he does not blink away. "Little suns"— this is what everyone calls them. The massive disks hover in the atmosphere, spilling streams of radiant light to the ground. The boy stares into the trees, mere meters from the door, and the forest encaving the unit stares back. A breeze finds him, whistling through the trees and into his dungarees. Threadbare with a Batman logo printed on them, the over-alls belonged to his mother when she was a child.

Peeling his hand off the latch, the boy steals into the bright night. He hurries into the bushes, steering clear of the stone-paved forest pathways, each step sending emerald grasshoppers chirping off the shrubs. In the forest, its canopy a roof of green, darkness collects in patches, but the lights find a way— they always do. Through holes in the dense cover of leaves, they pierce the dark, forming lines of shimmering mist. The trees above crash gently into each other, and the rains that had collected in them fall to the boy's skin in beaded drops. The musk of wet bark, bold and consuming, fills his nostrils as he weaves through the low-hanging palm fronds.

Before the light zones, the world had many green places — rainforests, savannas, mangroves— stretching as far as the eye could see. Not anymore. The Anambra Light Zone, with its damp places and its bird calls, is the only home the boy has ever known. He knows which months the leaves yellow and fall; he knows the poison mushrooms, their caps a vivid toxic scream. He knows the stones that birth the streams; he knows the places the Niger River breaks.

The boy stops when he sees the electric fence of the Multi-Science Research Facility, the words RESTRICTED AREA plastered across it in red. Made up of rows of cuboid structures, the facility stands at the west end of the light zone, with carpets of green algae crawling over it. When they were bored of tree counting, he and the other zone children would sometimes hide in the udala trees and guess at what might have once been the colour of the buildings.

"Vermilion." Kiki, who had a crack zipping across the lens of her glasses, always said the strangest things.

"That's not a color," some chunky kid laughed.

"Raymond, you thought peanut butter was mashed meat," she replied to the chunky kid without looking over at him. "Maybe sit this one out." She adjusted her glasses, fiddling with the duct tape that was doing a terrible job at holding the hinges in place.

"That was a long time ago!" Raymond looked around to the others, begging to be believed.

"Not long enough, apparently."

Nobody liked going river jumping or antelope watching with Kiki, and this was why. She didn't want them around either, but holed up in the zone together, they were stuck with each other.

✸ ✸ ✸

Thirteen years ago, in the eternal winter of 2125, the boy and Kiki had been born here. They went to the same zonal school, climbed the same trees, and chased the same squirrels.

But Kiki was not one for words, and when she was, the other children ran back to their units in tears. So when she leaned forward in history class and whispered into the boy's ear, "Meet me by the facility, under the udala trees," he thought she'd mistaken him for someone else. But she hadn't. "11 p.m. Don't be late."

"No talking," Mr. Adesua, the geography teacher who also doubled as the history teacher, warned the class, his narrowed eyes jailed behind thick oval spectacles. "Now, where were we?"

He turned to the holographic board. "...Yes, on the 14th of May, 2060, Mount Nyiragongo erupted in the Congo Basin, an eruption that spanned ten months. With increased steaming, rumbling aftershocks, and smoke emissions occurring for the next decade, it was the longest, most intense volcanic disaster after the 1815 eruption of...?"

Mr. Adesua looked around at his students— some doodling on their holo-pads, others fiddling with their glow pens, and only a precious few making an effort to feign attentiveness. "Anyone?"

"The 1815 eruption of Tambora in Indonesia."

"Thank you, Kiki," the teacher sighed, resuming his lecture. "With an endless fount of ash saturating the atmosphere and obscuring the sun, Africa, our continent, truly became The Dark Continent." A trail of dread crept into Mr. Adesua's voice. That same dread found its way onto the faces of his now-attentive students.

"Sulfuric acid aerosols increased the reflection of solar radiation across the globe. Rivers and lakes in Greenland froze over; in Russia, buildings, cities, and millions of people were entombed in ice. And for the first time since the Ice Age, equatorial regions experienced winter..."

The boy's attention drifted as he wondered what Kiki wanted with him. This was the first time she'd said more than a sentence to him. And though he made up his mind not to, he would later find himself hunching by the facility's fence, breaking curfew.

✸ ✸ ✸

Shifting his weight from one foot to the other, arms crossed tightly over his chest, the boy tries to stay hidden. An industrial-grade air filter thrums next to him, sending soft vibrations up his legs. With the incandescent "little suns" blazing bright, it is just a matter of time before the tight security team spots him.

Equipped with a self-regulating heat-yielding capability, the little suns warm frozen landscapes while simultaneously taking over the real sun's photosynthetic role. This made the Anambra Light Zone home to some of the last surviving biological species in Nigeria, as well as the rest of the planet— the reason it's heavily guarded by high-voltage walls against poachers and raiders from outside.

"Boy." The boy looks up to find Kiki hanging from a branch. "You're late." She lets go, and when her feet meet the ground, they do not make a sound.

"This doesn't feel right," the boy says, his breath quickening. "Let's—"

"There's no security on this side. I checked." She takes his hand. "Come."

They slink onto the Facility grounds through a rip in the wired fence and head towards one of its many buildings. At the entrance, Kiki slips out a key card. She slides it across the door-lock, and it buzzes open, revealing an empty hallway.

"My dads work here," she explains, catching the questioning look on the boy's face. "Research biologists."

Half-tiptoeing, half-running, hand in hand, they hurry down the hall. The walls on each side are large glass panes, and behind them are laboratories full of things the boy has seen only in books —microscopes, Petri dishes, titration filters, jars with brownish stuff floating in them— and, in some of the rooms, things not in the boy's books.

Kiki whirls around. "What are you doing?" His hand has slipped from hers.

The boy leaves her to peer through one of the glass panes. "Is that a—?"

"Yes. A prototype. Let's go." She pulls on the strap of his overalls, but he does not budge.

"I want to see it."

"You're seeing it now."

"Up close." He goes to the door, and Kiki knows she's not winning this one.

"I am so going to regret bringing you here." She swipes the key card across the lock. Inside, a little sun fills the room. Far from what the boy imagined, it is not flat but cylindrical, like a bass drum, and insanely massive. And there is nothing ethereal about it. Wires, plugs, and circuits jot out from within it, like twigs on a dying tree. He runs his finger along its dusty metal exterior.

Kiki stiffens where she stands. "We need to go."

With its two surfaces —one plated with blue solar cells, the other made of columns of fluorescent tubes— the little sun is in practice a solar-powered streetlight, only larger and more complex.

"How does it work?"

"I. Don't. Know." Kiki punctuates every word, exasperation working into her voice.

But of course she knows. Unlike the boy, she paid attention in Introductory Tech class. To fight the climate crisis, world governments invented the "little suns." The disks, a hundred times more powerful than the average solar panel, absorb light energy from the sun, converting it to beams too concentrated for the sulfuric aerosols in the atmosphere to reflect. And so, dusk till dawn, the little suns shine, sentries on guard.

"Woah." The boy looks up. A map is etched into the ceiling. "Is that a world map?"

"More like a map of what's left. Come on. Let's go."

"What are those? The red spots?"

"Light zones."

"So few?" He slants his head. "Why couldn't they just shield the whole world?" He gestures to the prototype.

"Do you ever listen in class?"

The boy shrugs.

"With limited time and resources, the advanced multi-purpose billion-dollar design of the technology was not accessible enough to enclose entire countries," Kiki starts like she's reading out of an encyclopedia. The boy blinks at her. "A compromise was reached, and the suns were suspended over arable lands, wildlife reserves, and forests."

"Monaco did it." The boy smirks, crossing his arms. He knows something she doesn't.

"Monaco was a very small, very wealthy nation," Kiki sighs. "They could afford to shield their entire landmass."

The boy looks back up. The area above the US and its five zones is a sheer patch of white. "Mr. Adesua said Canada was a frozen graveyard long before a little sun got mounted."

"The aftermath of the eruption was hardest on polar countries. Most had to migrate their citizens towards the equator, to Kenya, Indonesia, Colombia, and here. Sure, it's cold here, but it's tolerable."

"Do you think the people on the outside are okay?"

"Seeing as they're always trying to get in here, I take it they're not."

"We should just let them in."

"We— We can't."

"Why?"

"There's barely enough room and resources as it is. We can't risk an overpopulation crisis. Our parents are only here because the work they do is important, nothing more."

"My mum doesn't work here in the facility like your parents. She's down in agriculture."

"And without her, we'd all starve, including those on the outside relying on us for monthly supplies." Kiki takes his hand again. "I want to show you something."

✺ ✺ ✺

They head to the end of the hall and down a spiraling metal staircase. The stairs empty into a mass of interlocking pipes and dripping tanks that comprise the central grid of the drainage system. A chemical stench hangs in the air.

Kiki lifts a sewage lid like she's done it a hundred times before, and the lights spill past her, into the dark below. "Get in."

"No." The boy backs away. "I'm not jumping into some random sewer." His astonishment at seeing the prototype is long gone at this point. "I knew I should never have come."

"So why did you?"

"I don't know. I thought maybe you— I don't know." He coughs once, scratching the side of his neck.

"Oh god, you thought I wanted to kiss you?" Kiki's expression cannot decide between disgust and shock.

"Ye— No— That's not what I meant."

"Just get in."

Too embarrassed to protest further, the boy climbs down the greasy wet ladder. Following him, Kiki closes the lid, and the sewer goes pitch black. In the forest, under the cover of the canopy, the boy has experienced shades of darkness, but nothing like this. This is encompassing, ripping him of his sense of space, of being. He cannot tell where his body ends and where the darkness begins.

"Kiki, where are you?!"

"Relax, I'm right here." She shines a headlamp in his face.

"I want to go back."

"Not yet." Handing him a lamp from the row of others hanging on the sewer wall, she trudges ahead, dispatching puddles of water with every step. The boy follows. Walking with a knowing sway, Kiki does not pause when the tunnel splits in three, and —unlike the boy— does not shriek when a rat scurries over her toes.

"How many times have you been down here?"

"Hm," Kiki mutters, and nothing else.

The air starts to smell of river rocks as the pipes, mucky water, and defined walls give way to a larger, rough, cave-like exterior. Kiki stops.

The boy bumps into her. "Are we there?"

"Turn it off," she says, switching her lamp off. "They don't like the light."

"Who?" The boy hesitantly does as she says. "Who doesn't like the—" Then he sees it: a speck of light afloat in the dark. Another follows, twirling and glinting, up and up. A third comes, then a fourth, then a thousand.

"Fire— Fireflies." The word leaves his lips as a whisper, his breath catching in his throat.

"Have you ever seen anything like it?" The swirling lights glint off the lenses of Kiki's glasses, casting her entire face in a scintillating glow.

In the cave's immensity, swelling with the euphonic hum of lacy wings, swarms of fireflies dance, a rain of stars. No, the boy has seen nothing like it.

"But..." He finds his voice. "My mum said... She said they all disappeared when she was little. She said the lights blinded them. She said—"

"I know, I know. The lights made their mating glow invisible and, unable to evade predators or reproduce, they went extinct. I know." Kiki lets her impatience show. "But look, they're right here!"

"How did you find them?"

"I didn't. My dads have been coming down here for months, studying them, how they've survived this long."

"I guess the warmth from the little suns helped." The boy inhales the fresh warm air.

"About that…"

"What?"

"Don't freak out, but we're not in the zone anymore."

"Where— Where are we?"

"Where do you think?" Kiki scoffs.

It takes a minute, but it comes to the boy. His eyes widening, he spins around, frantic.

"No, no, this is a good thing." She reaches for his shoulders. "We're outside the zone, but it's not freezing down here. Don't you see what that means?"

"We can't— We can't possibly be that far away?"

"We've been walking for hours." She beeps her timepiece in his face. "It's 6 a.m." The boy gasps. "I'm usually faster on my own, but thanks to your side quests, we are definitely getting caught. Point is, the earth is healing," Kiki says, her voice charged with something the boy cannot describe.

"My dads say soon we might not need the little suns anymore."

"Really? How soon?"

"They're not sure." She pauses for a minute. "But can you imagine? Seeing the oceans, a sunset, the moon!" Her hands tighten around his shoulders, and she shakes him. "Boy!"

"Zaram."

Kiki raises a brow.

"My name is Zaram." The boy stares down at his fingers.

"And all this while I thought it was 'Boy.'" She lets out a mocking chuckle. "I know."

Zaram looks up at the fireflies. "Kiki, why— Why did you pick me?"

She does not look at him, but not in the same way that she doesn't look at the other zone children, like Raymond. "Well, out of everyone here… I hate you the least." A shy humming silence builds in the space between them. "What would you like to see, Zaram, when the earth is normal again?"

"I— I—" He has never thought about it. This —the light zone, the little suns— is his normal.

"It's alright," Kiki smiles. "You don't have to think about it now."

Zaram smiles back. And they stay, watching all the little things daring to shine. 🜚

Like Stars Daring to Shine was originally published in Fireside Magazine in July, 2021

Somto Ihezue

THE RAINMAKERS

BY MEGAN M. DAVIES-OSTROM

"When in doubt—" I catch Thomas's eyes and hold up a jar of sparkle lip gloss. "—add more glitter."

The mirror we face is cracked and wreathed in vanity lights that flicker in time with the strained chugging of the ancient generator outside. The smells of old perfume, road dust, and hush-puppies fill the painted wooden wagon that serves triple duty as my transportation, home, and dressing room. I blame the generator for that last odour. We restocked on biodiesel at our last stop, and now everything smells like frying corn.

"It's your go-to, glitter. You can never have too much."

Thomas nods and bends over the worn, hand-stitched journal he carries everywhere. "Glitter," he whispers, as his stub of pencil scratches across the page.

"But first things first." I trade the lip gloss for a facecloth and hand a second to Thomas. "We've got to cleanse, glue down those bushy man-brows, prime, colour-correct, and girl…conceal, conceal, conceal."

We pulled into Sweet Spring at sunset, and from my perch on the box of my wagon I got a prime view of the colours —reds, oranges, and purples— sweeping the saffron-yellow sky above the mesas.

Sweet Spring was a little place, not much more than a few farms and a trading post, but it was neat and in good repair. That always boded well. It looked like the whole town had turned out to greet us. Women, men, and children in their much-mended and wash-thinned best lined the rough dirt road, waving and cheering as we drew near. A little girl with dark braids ran forward and threw flowers on the path in front of us. She giggled when one of my mules bent low to snatch them up. Good ol' Harvey, he was never one to turn down a treat. And who was I to begrudge him? The roads through the Dry between New Angeles and Sweet Spring were long, hot, and nasty. Narrow, hard-scrabble tracks through rough terrain where water and food were scarce, and good people were scarcer still. They were dangerous, those roads. Easy to get lost and starve, easy to run into trouble. Roving bands of Haters liked to ambush the weak and unwary out there on those roads. They *usually* avoided travelling Rainmakers, but people like that are rando, and we'd pushed hard to cover the distance quickly. Harvey was one tired mule, and he deserved his treat.

We came to a stop in the dirt square at the centre of town and tied up at the hitching posts there. We'd tend to our chores —unharnessing, grooming, feeding— once the formalities were over with.

Here the town leaders —both official and otherwise— awaited us. Faces young and old, stamped with a mixed bag of emotions; hope, interest, uncertainty. My eyes slid past them all, drawn immediately to the small, white-haired woman who stood by the edge of the group. A sturdy, well-built young man sat on a wooden crate in front of her, staring up at me with curious eyes. The woman wasn't big or particularly well dressed, and her face was creased with wrinkles that spoke of many long years between the yellow skies and sand, but her presence had weight. Everything about her —from the tight twist of her bun to the firm hand resting on the young man's shoulder— radiated authority. I didn't know if she held any official title, but there was no doubt she was in charge. She was the one who'd sent for us, I was sure of it.

When my fellow Rainmakers, sixteen of us in all, had assembled, I bowed to the woman.

"Emma Allen, I presume?"

She nodded, a short, sharp movement. "The same. Glad to see someone got our message. Took y'all long enough to get here."

The young man gasped, but I laughed. I liked people who spoke their minds, especially little old ladies. Show me a feisty old girl dishing shade, and my mind immediately went to my old drag mother, Fifi Foxxx. Now, Fifi— she'd been a Queen, full of pride, sass, and determination. Emma Allen was the same. No candle to Fifi in looks or glam, obviously, but the attitude? Hells yes.

"All's well that ends well, I s'pose," she allowed. "Welcome to Sweet Spring, Rainmakers."

"The pleasure's ours. Thank you for your hospitality." I gestured to the young man who sat before her. "Is this the boy you wrote about?"

She nodded again and nudged the young man to his feet. He was handsome enough, with clear skin, bright, wide-set eyes, and a full set of teeth. There was a resemblance to Emma in those features. A grandson, perhaps, or great-nephew? Potential, too. He had good *bones*. But did he have what it took to be a Rainmaker? Of that, I wasn't sure.

"This is Thomas, my grandson. Turned seventeen last planting, but he's had the calling long as I can remember. He's a Rainmaker through an' through."

If I had a sequin for every time I'd heard that, I'd glitter like a diamond.

According to folklore, having a Rainmaker in the family was lucky. You'd be blessed, the stories said, with fertile land and bountiful crops. You'd be fertile and bountiful too, the whispers added. From a purely practical perspective, a Rainmaker's hometown got priority when it came time to call down the clouds. Out here in the Dry, where one rainstorm could spell the difference between famine and plenty, that meant something. I'd seen all sorts of unsuitable candidates put forward by desperate people hoping to change their luck.

"We'll see." I offered Thomas my hand and received a firm shake in return. He had working hands, rough and strong. No surprise there. He was a farm-boy from head to toe. Strong wasn't a problem. Rainmaking could be hard labour, and there was always room for someone who knew their way around livestock. Rough, on the other hand, was an issue. A Queen always took care of her skin. If we took him on, that skin would need fixing.

"Hello, Thomas. When I'm Rainmaking, I'm Clementine Devine, and I go by her and she, but right now you can call me Clem and him/he is fine. Tell me about this calling of yours. Why do you think you're meant to be Rainmaker?"

"Well, Queen—"

"Clem is just fine, when I'm out of drag."

"Well, Clem, I think I've just always known, ever since I first saw a troupe of Rainmakers come to town when I was a little sprout. I want to help people. Be useful, make sure they've got what they need. That's what Rainmakers do, isn't it? Help people and spread the love?"

"That it is. But being a Rainmaker isn't easy, Thomas. If we accepted you, it would mean leaving all this behind; your town, your family, your friends. It would mean travelling all around the Dry, fending for ourselves and making do. Sometimes we go weeks between towns."

"I can do that, sir. I'm strong, and Gran says I'm smart enough. I'm used to doing my share."

"What about fighting? Can you do that? There are Haters out there, and they don't always respect the rainbow flag."

"Can't say as I've had any experience with fighting, sir, but I'm willing to try. An' I've hunted a fair bit… I'm a good shot with the rifle."

He seemed a fine lad, open and hard-working. But that wasn't good enough. If it were just hard work —travelling between communities, delivering messages, medicines, and goods, helping out, lending a hand— then any sensible young man would have fit the bill. But Rainmaking was something more, and very few had what it took.

"What about the other side of it? The Rainmaking? Can you put on the drag? Can you dance and sing in front of a whole town to call down the clouds and the rains?" This was the question that counted. If he hadn't really heard the call, this would be where it would show. I had yet to meet a boy who could fool me.

"I can do that too, Qu— Clem." No hesitation. "I know my build ain't great for it, what with my shoulders an' all, but I'll do my very best. An'…" His gaze dropped for a moment. When he looked up again, his eyes were filled with a longing I knew all too well. "An' I want to glitter, Queen. I want to shine."

A perfect answer, and a real one too, by my guess. Certainly good enough to let him try. He had the calling all right, but only time would tell if he had the skills. Not everyone was cut out to be a Rainmaker.

Megan M. Davies-Ostrom

"Once you've got a nice, smooth surface, it's time to contour." I apply highlights and shadows to my own face and then help Thomas with his, showing him how to accentuate his cheekbones and soften his square chin.

"Me, I've got a right big schnozz, so I like to go in with a lot of highlighter on the bridge and tip to snatch it in. Yours is narrower, so we shouldn't have as much to do there."

"What if I make a mess of things?" Thomas' voice trembles with nervous energy. Fear too, I imagine. "What if I forget the words or the routines?"

A Rainmaker's first performance is always the hardest, and despite all his strengths, Thomas is no different. He's as jittery as a spring kid, glancing at the door and jumping at every sound.

"Not likely, given the way you've been practicing. And even if you do, it's not a big deal."

He stares at me, a look of horror on his half-baked face. "Not a big deal? How can you say that? Those songs are tradition. What if I screw up, an' the clouds don't come, or if—"

"They'll come. Yeah, the songs and dances we perform are tradition, but the real magic's in the intent. If you put your heart and soul into it —dance for your life and spread the love—the rains will know, and they'll come."

"But how can you be sure?"

"'Cause I've been doing this almost my whole life, Thomas, and that's more years than I'll ever say out loud. I've seen all sorts of mess-ups and missed steps, but I've never seen the rains stay away. If we dance, they'll come."

We left Sweet Spring late the next morning, after delivering a sack of dusty, well-travelled letters, helping repair the generator at the Trading Post, and swapping some sheet metal for corn meal, cooking oil, and five precious jars of powdered mineral pigments. Mixed with jojoba oil, beeswax, witch hazel, and clay, they'd become concealer, blush, eyeshadow, and lipstick.

Thomas hugged his parents and grandmother goodbye, and promised to write often. He exchanged tearful embraces with a young man and woman as well. The rest of the troupe bent our attention to harnessing our mules and gave him his privacy. It was never easy to leave home and the ones you loved. Leaving to become a Rainmaker was harder still. We travelled the Dry for months on end, stopping in towns along the way to lend a hand as needed or call down the clouds. A few days here, a week there, never long enough in one place to find love or form attachments. Being a Rainmaker could be a lonely life. Could be, but didn't have to be. If those young folk loved him, they'd be patient and welcome him back with open arms when the turns of the seasons brought us this way again.

From Sweet Spring we travelled south. Thomas shared with Milo, who had the biggest wagon and acted as drag mother for our troupe. It was Milo's job to show newbies the ropes and start them learning the songs and dances for calling down the clouds and the rains. When and if we were sure Thomas was staying, we'd trade for what we needed to build him a wagon of his own.

Thomas was eager to learn and full of questions. Only good manners —hammered into him by his grandmother, I imagined— kept him from peppering us all day long. On the second day I took pity and invited him to ride with me and ask anything he liked.

He asked about where we were headed (south to Tumbleweed and beyond) and how long it would take to reach our first stop (seven or eight days, if the weather held). He asked about make-up (lots) and costuming (sparkly) and where we got our wigs (donated hair and very fine craftspeople in New Angeles). Finally, after a few moments of pensive silence, he asked "Why did you become a Rainmaker, Clem?"

I knew he'd ask eventually, and I'd already thought about what I'd say. I'd learned over the years that while everyone asked, not everyone was comfortable with the answer. Thomas was a steady lad; he'd be one of the ones who could handle the real story. Still, best to give him a choice about it.

"Do you want the easy answer, or the real one? Real one's not pretty, just saying. A bit TMI for some people."

He studied my face for a moment. "Both, if that's okay with you."

"I wouldn't have offered if it wasn't. The easy answer's that I heard the call, just like everyone else here in the troupe. It's true, too, for what it's worth. One of my first memories is of sitting in the back of my father's truck and holding an old wedding dress he'd…found. 'Keep it off the bed and keep it clean,' he told me, 'or I'll whip you till you bleed.' He meant it too, so I held that dress all bunched up on my lap as if were the most precious thing on earth, and the whole time, all I could do was stare at it. It was the prettiest thing I'd ever seen, all lace and sparkle and little beads that caught the sun coming through the dirty windows and glittered like rainbows. I wanted that dress more than I'd ever wanted anything in my life. I wanted to own it and wear it and make it my second skin. I wanted to *be* that dress, if that makes sense."

"It makes perfect sense. I felt the same way when Callie —that's my older sister— got married a couple a' years ago. She looked so pretty, and all I wanted was to try on her dress. Wouldn't a' fit me, a' course. But still…" He paused a moment, eyes closed in reminiscence. "What about the other answer, the too-much-info one? Is it something bad?"

"Yeah, it is. For some people, it's unforgivable. And I understand why. Even when you spend your whole life learning to spread the love, sometimes it's hard to forgive."

"What do you mean? Did you hurt someone?"

"No, not me, not directly. But my parents did. My parents were Haters."

Thomas's eyes widened, but he didn't flinch or gasp. "What happened?"

"What always happens with Haters. They attacked and people died. Haters learn the opposite of spreading the love. They believe in looking out for number one, and taking what they want, and survival of the strongest. To grow up a Hater is thinking the world's made of fear and greed and pain. That's what I was taught when I was little. I didn't know there was anything else till the day I saw that wedding dress and realized the world held beauty too. I wanted that beauty in my life, and I got my chance the day our band attacked a troupe of Rainmakers."

"They attacked Rainmakers?" Now there was horror in his voice.

"They did. My father was a Big Man in our band, second only to the Boss. He was tough and macho and full of ego. No matter what anyone else did, he had to do it bigger and better. When his chief rival for the Boss's favor raided a fat trade caravan, my father needed an even bigger prize. I guess he figured Rainmakers would be just the thing. I was around ten years old, and he brought me with him. I was old enough to fight, and he wanted me to be a Big Man too."

"Did he kill them?"

"Are you kidding? Hells no! Rainmakers are always more than they seem, you should know that. Not saying he didn't do *damage*, but when the bullets stopped flying, most of the Rainmakers were still standing, and my father's raiding party were dead in the sand."

"What about you?"

"I was the only survivor. They found me hidden under the seat of my father's truck, all ragged and feral and covered in scars. They were scared of me, at first. I can imagine what must have been going through their minds. How could such a child understand any show of kindness? How could such a child learn to spread to the love? They debated whether to leave me behind or take me to the closest town. I asked if could stay with them instead."

"What did they say?"

"When the clamor and kerfuffle died down, not much. They were too surprised. Finally, one of them —a big, round man who I later learned to call Philip when he was off stage and Fifi when she was on— asked me why.

"'Cause your clothes and your wagons are so pretty.' I was sobbing, too scared and desperate to be tough. My father would'a beat me silly if he'd seen, but he was dead in the dust, and for the first time in my life, I could speak my mind. 'Like the wedding dress an' the flowers an' the pretty girls. I want to be pretty too!'

"And that was it. They took me in. Taught me to spread love instead of hate, and to dance and sing the clouds down. Some people don't like to hear my story, because they've lost family to Haters, or been hurt themselves. I guess it's easier to be angry when what you're angry at isn't the same as you at all. I make them think. It makes them uncomfortable."

"Well it shouldn't. They should be relieved."

"Why do you say that?"

"Because your story proves that hate isn't bred into the blood and bones. That it's taught and learned. And if it can be learned, it can be unlearned too. Maybe someday there'll be no more Haters at all."

That was my dream too.

Once our faces are done, I help Thomas with his wig. Milo gave him free run of the extras, and he's chosen a cascade of loose brown curls that fall to the centre of his back. It's an interesting choice for a newb, nowhere near as flashy as blond or red, but the moment it's on, I know he's made the perfect choice.

"Beautiful." I hand him some bobby pins. "It's beautiful. The highlights bring out the colour of your eyes."

He smiles a shy smile and gazes in wonder at his reflection in the mirror. "I look like Callie." He laughs. "Only with better cheekbones."

"That's the spirit!"

I rise, fetch the garment bags from their hooks on the door, and hand one to Thomas. "Best for last. Here's your dress."

He takes the bag in loving hands and slides the zipper down a few inches to reveal the masterpiece of vintage silver satin and Swarovski inside.

"It's a classic, passed down from Rainmaker to Rainmaker for I don't know how long. Last one to wear it was Fifi, and I've been saving it for just the right Queen. Now it's yours. I've altered it; it should you fit just right."

Thomas pauses mid-zip and stares up at me. "But Clem… wow, I…I don't know what to say. Thank you! I mean—"

"No thanks necessary. You just wear it and shine. You'll do great."

We stayed two nights in the town called Tumbleweed and a week in Cottonwood Creek. What with planting season still a month off, we did whatever was needed and traded chores for our food, fuel, and water. Milo was a blacksmith, Finn had trained to be a doctor before he heard the call, and Isla could sheer a sheep in three minutes flat. Thomas made himself useful too, chopping firewood, digging post-holes, and doing just about anything else we asked. He wasn't afraid of hard work, and he had a quiet, earnest charm that put people at ease.

But was he a Rainmaker?

Of that, we still weren't sure.

We stopped along the road for rehearsals, out in the Dry where there was no one to see but ourselves. Thomas picked up the songs and dances quick enough, but as for performance, he lacked the *je ne sais quoi* that made a *true* Rainmaker.

"You need to be more confident," Milo told him. "Smile, sashay."

"Make sure you're well rested before rehearsal," Mia suggested. "Have a snack."

"Picture success," Finn said. "Positive thoughts only."

Thomas tried it all, but there was still something missing.

"Give him time," I told Milo. "Give him time. Some people just need the right push to glow-up."

We were two weeks out of Cottonwood Creek and five days shy of Kéyah when the Haters attacked. They caught us by surprise in a narrow valley between two high bluffs, the perfect place for an ambush. Mia and Ezra had been riding scout, but they'd given no warning. That meant one thing. They were dead, outnumbered and overwhelmed before they could raise the alarm. If we didn't fight back hard and fast, the rest of us would follow.

The way was too narrow for us to turn and flee, and there was nowhere to hide as the bullets and arrows rained down on us.

"Take cover!" I yelled.

Wild screams and curses echoed down from the crevices and shadows of the boulder-strewn slopes above us. Howling, foul, violent language, promises of pain and torture. I'd known those words once, had shouted them myself and watched our victims —innocent farmers and traders— cringe in fear. Not this time. We were Queens, Rainmakers, and we wouldn't be intimidated.

"Take cover and return fire!"

"At what?" Thomas gasped as he grabbed his rifle and ducked behind the seat. "I can't see them!"

It was typical Hater strategy. They'd stay hidden and pick us off one by one. It would work too, unless we changed the game.

I grabbed the rainbow flag mounted next to my seat and jumped down. "Aim for the ridgeline and the shadows." I ran to the middle of the dusty road. "They'll show themselves. I'll make them."

I waved the flag above my head and screamed at the hills. "Hey you, Big Man. Where are you? I know you're up there! Show yourself."

"What's he doing?" Thomas cried. "Clem don't be crazy, get back here!"

"No, he's right," Milo hissed. "Just wait. Haters are macho; they can't resist a challenge. He's going to draw the Big Man out."

I smiled a thin, fierce smile, and waved the flag harder. I'd grown up in that world, surrounded by that toxic fear and insecurity. Milo understood.

"Come on, you big coward," I yelled. "I'm right here! What kind of leader are you? Hiding like a frightened child. Come and face me, if you've got the balls for it! Face me like a real warrior!"

A roar of angry denial echoed from the shadows on the ridge to my right as a beefy man broke cover and rushed me like an enraged bull. He went down in a short, sharp rattle of rifle-fire. Simple, predictable, sad. Big Men were all the same.

Now for the iffy part.

"Your Big Man is dead," I called to the darkened hills. "If you lay down your weapons and leave, we'll let you live. If you fight, you'll die."

We gave them a chance, because violence was the opposite of spreading the love.

We gave them a chance, but they didn't take it. Haters almost never do.

They screamed and cursed and poured down the slopes in a blood-thirsty, blade-swinging wave.

We cut them down.

Like I'd said to Thomas, Rainmakers are always more than they seem. We trained every day, and once they'd shown themselves, the Haters stood no chance.

When the last of the Haters had fallen, I found Thomas behind the wagon-seat with tears streaking his dusty cheeks.

"I'm so sorry Clem, I couldn't do it! I tried to shoot, but all I could see was their eyes. They're people just like us! How can people hate so much? And how can I kill em' without becoming just like em'?"

I wrapped my arms around him and held him close. "It's okay, Thomas. It was your first real fight. Shooting a real person's harder than a target. And that's love holding you back. Never apologize for love."

We searched the slopes and the hills beyond for survivors. We found a little girl, no more than four or five, huddled behind a boulder with the body of her mother. She hissed and spat at us as we approached and scrabbled for a rock to use as a weapon.

"She's just a baby." Thomas' face was pale. "No bigger than my littlest sister. How could anyone bring a baby to a fight like this?"

"Hate's learned young," I replied.

Thomas knelt and smiled that soft smile of his. "It's okay, little one. We're not going to hurt you. You're safe with us." He offered his hand and much to my surprise, she set down her rock and came to him. He scooped her up and carried her back to our wagons, away from the carnage.

That evening we piled the bodies, over twenty in all, beside the road, and set Mia and Ezra, who we'd found hidden in a gully with their throats slit, alongside them. Rainmaker or Hater, in death we're all the same. We gathered brush and dry grasses and made a pyre, and when it was burning high, we sang the long farewell. Familiar voices, familiar song. We'd sung it before, and I had no doubt we'd sing it again. Such was life in the Dry.

But as I sang and watched the flames dance, a new voice joined the rest, strong and clear. It slipped along the edges of the song, adding harmony and depth. Adding layers of meaning that cut to the core.

This is grief, the voice sang, for lives lost and lives wasted. This is pain and desolation. But this is promise too. Of redemption and fortitude and a chance at a new tomorrow where no one learns to hate.

Heart tight, I spun to find the source of that voice. Thomas sat a few feet away with the little Hater girl on his knees. His eyes were closed, his face tilted to the sky and cheeks wet with tears, and he was singing for all he was worth.

I'd told Milo that sometimes it just took the right impetus for someone to find their sparkle. Thomas had found his. Helping real people, doing real good; it brought out the Queen in him like no amount of practice ever could. He was a Rainmaker for sure.

"Would it be okay…that is, my Gran gave me some of her jewelry before I left, and I was wondering—"

"Yes Thomas, you can wear your Gran's jewelry." I slide the glittering chain from the faded velvet box in her hands and fasten it around her neck. "Perfect. Now you're a Queen."

She turns and looks in the mirror once more, letting her breath out in a shaky sigh.

"Wow. I never imagined I could look like this. I'm so happy, Clementine."

"Use it. Take that feeling in your heart and share it with everyone out there."

I clip on my own earrings and slide my feet into my size twelve rhinestone heels. Like Thomas's dress, they're precious, passed down through the generations since before the sky was yellow and the earth dry.

It's a short walk from where we set up the wagons to the town square, and we blow kisses to the crowd as we go. The traditional cheers of "Yaaaas, Queen!" and "You go, girl!" echo off the hills and fill the dull yellow sky with startled birds. Soon we'll fill that sky with clouds, and then the rains will come and the crops will grow.

We take our places. Milo, as Raspberry De-Light is on my left, and Thomas, as the newly minted Miss Love O'Plenty, on my right. I give Miss Love a grin.

"Ready?"

"Not really, but let's do this thing anyway!"

The music starts, and we dance and sing, beginning, as always, with "It's Raining Men." Miss Love's voice rings out clearer, stronger, and more powerful than it ever was in rehearsals. As strong as it was in grief, and just as beautiful.

The skies open and the rains fall. We dance, sing, and glitter along with the deluge.

Rainmaking is a thing of beauty, and joy lights the wet faces of the crowd, including the little girl who's become Miss Love's constant shadow. She isn't the first orphan to be raised by Rainmakers, and she won't be the last. Her smile makes my heart happy.

Joy is a form of love, just like sorrow, compassion, and hope. Just like a child's smile or raindrops on the dry ground.

Spread the love; it's what Rainmakers do.

"The Rainmakers" was originally published in Fantasy Magazine Issue # 74, December 2021.

LOST IN INTUITION
BY AMARA MESNIK

When the self-driving cab pulled away from the quaint farmhouse-style home, Monica knew she was stranded. She couldn't call it back. She couldn't order another. The only way now was forward.

Monica took a breath, then hiked up the porch stairs and knocked on the regal wooden door. Once. Twice. No response.

She glanced around to see if any neighbors were spying. It had been ages since she'd been in the suburbs, and she'd forgotten just how *green* everything was in late spring. It was like a painting made of neon Jello-shot vomit. Birds were flitting through the trees, teasing her with merry songs, while squirrels chittered in the branches, waving their feather-boa tails like the high-society cousins of the big city's rats. Even the nature out here was elitist. Monica wouldn't have been surprised if the chipmunks' stripes were designer.

No one was looking, so she knocked again.

This time, muffled footsteps brought acid to her throat.

Don't open, don't open...

The door swung open. Julia looked her up and down, taking in the bags in her arms and the boxes on the sidewalk.

"You could've called."

Monica pulled out a plastic baggie containing the shattered remnants of her phone. "Not really."

"Things with Mike went sideways?"

Julia didn't sound too heartbroken about it. Monica wasn't surprised. But she was far too sober for an 'I told you so'.

The words she needed to say clung to her tongue like bonded magnets, but she managed to push them out.

"Can I come in?"

In the front sitting room —sorry, the *parlor*— Monica raised an eyebrow as she accepted the teacup her sister offered. It was pink and flowery, just like everything in Julia's house.

"Brandon doesn't mind living in *The Secret Garden*?" Monica asked as Julia poured the tea. She watched the steam rise in lazy rivulets.

"No, he thinks it's nice," said Julia, setting the kettle onto a little copper stand on the table. "Do you even know what *The Secret Garden* is about?"

"A garden? I dunno. Never read it."

"There's a copy on the bookshelf if you'd like to, now that you've got the time."

Monica hid an eye roll behind a sip of tea.

The two sisters steeped in the silence for a long moment before Julia asked, "Do you want to talk about it?"

Monica scoffed. "Do you really care?"

"I do, Nicky. I always have."

Monica's fingers tightened on the teacup's handle. Julia had always been like this— acting like she'd been right all along, pretending to care. She had the better job, more money, a perfect family; of course she knew best. It was all so self-serving.

"I'd rather not get into it."

Julia shrugged. "Well, I told Brandon you'd be staying a few days. You can take the guest room, though you'll have to move Summer's toys. It's become her playroom."

Monica tried to do some math to figure out how old her niece was, but her thoughts fizzled out. "Thank you."

Julia studied her for a moment. "Were you expecting me to put up more of a fight?"

The question was unexpected. Monica thought about it. She almost wished she had. Maybe then it wouldn't feel like she'd hit rock bottom. It would just feel like old times.

In the morning, Monica woke up to a pair of round blue eyes staring right into her soul. She sucked in a breath and sat up. It was a little girl, maybe seven years old, in a bright pink cowgirl hat.

Summer squinted. "Who are you?"

"I'm your aunt," Monica said. "Your mom never showed you a picture of me?"

"No. Have you always been my aunt?"

"Yes, I've always been your aunt."

"Are you sure?"

"Summer!" came Julia's shout from down the hall. A moment later, she poked her head into the room. "Oh, *Summer*. Sorry, Nicky, she'll be off to school in a sec. Then I'll call you a car to the cell store. Alright? There's breakfast downstairs in the autobaker, help yourself." With that, she wrestled the protesting cowgirl out of the room.

Monica sat for a moment. It wasn't like they lived in the same town or city, and she hadn't attended a family get-together in years. It was perfectly understandable that Summer hadn't recognized her. So why did it make her heart sink?

She got dressed and sat on the porch until the self-driven school bus came and went, whisking Summer off to learn her ABCs, or whatever kids her age were doing these days. Everything was so safe now that the country had switched over to a fully autonomous system. The smart vehicles and ever-improving computers had all but eliminated accidents, and the tens of thousands of annual road deaths had diminished to near zero. Monica was certainly pleased to have her hands off the wheel; she'd never been the best at paying attention to where she was going.

"You've got the address?" Julia asked as she loaded up the car-calling app.

Monica held up the scrap of paper she'd written the cell store's details on. So old-fashioned.

"I'll see you later then. I make dinner at 5." Julia stepped back inside and closed the door.

Monica turned to face the street and closed her eyes. Dinner at 5. All she could imagine was herself sitting at the dinner table, eating mac and cheese out of a bright pink bowl just like Summer. Was this her life, now?

The car came within two minutes, a nice newer-model single-seater with a sunroof. Monica clambered inside, but as she did so, a not-so-gentle breeze suddenly tugged the paper out of her hand.

"No! Come back!" she exclaimed as the address fluttered away and out of sight, but she couldn't get out of the car to chase it without forfeiting the vehicle to another caller. And the thought of banging on Julia's door, telling her what had happened, and begging her to order another…

Monica pressed her head into her hands. Of course, this would happen to her. Of course, it would happen today, of all days, when she didn't even have a phone.

But did she need a smart phone when she was in a smart car?

Monica tapped on the screen impatiently before it lit up.

"Welcome to Moirai, your personalized car service. Please select manual, compound, or intuitive entry."

Monica groaned. Some new model. Who needed all these options?

"Intuitive, I guess." She hoped that meant easy mode.

The screen made a cheerful little chirp, then went to a login screen. "Please enter your Standard Access credentials to continue."

"Oh, come on," Monica muttered, tapping in her information on the keyboard it provided.

The car made a polite ping. "Successfully connected to Standard Access profile. Your search history has loaded. Please put on your seatbelt." A little GPS map appeared onscreen, previewing the route.

Monica blinked. "But I didn't put in an address…"

It didn't seem to matter, because the moment her seatbelt clicked, the car sped off.

Fine, Monica thought, figuring it had found the search she'd done for the cell store on Julia's computer. Maybe there was something to be said for the Standard Access system. It already knew where she needed to go.

Or not.

Ten minutes later, Monica found herself cursing under her breath as the car slowed in front of an all-too familiar house. And worse, when it stopped right in front of the old man mowing the lawn, who immediately cut the motor and squinted.

"Nicky? Is that you?"

Monica blanched. "Hi, dad."

Ryan dusted off his hands as he came up to the window, limping slightly. His hair had gone white and the lines in his face had deepened since she last saw him. Had it really been that long?

"I wish you would've called, your mother's out right now…"

"I'm not here to stay. I'm just passing through."

Ryan tilted his body, peering into the car. "Where's Mike?"

Monica ground her teeth. The last thing she wanted to do was explain the situation to her ex's biggest critic. Last time they'd visited, Mike had ended up at a hotel after her father had called him a scumbag, and Mike had called her father worse.

"He's gone."

"Ah. Just like that?"

"He cheated. I kicked him out. Then he reminded me he owned the place."

"Right. This was last night?"

"Yesterday morning."

"Where did you stay last night?"

"With Julia."

Ryan nodded. "Good. That's… that's good."

"I didn't burn the place down, if that's what you think."

"That's not— I'm just happy you saw her as a place to go for help."

The word made Monica cringe. "Yeah." It wasn't like there was anywhere else for her to go.

Ryan managed something of a friendly smile. "Well, you're always welcome here."

Now that Mike's out of the picture? Monica wanted to grumble. But instead, she just said, "Thanks."

Her father didn't seem to know how to back out of the conversation, so he stuck his hands into his pockets. "So… what's your plan?"

"Right now, I'm going to get a new phone. After that… I'm not sure."

"Well, kiddo, you'll figure it out. You always do." Ryan's smile lines furrowed. Then he started patting his pockets. "You got a pen on you by any chance?"

Confused, Monica pulled out the one she'd used earlier. She passed it through the window to her father, who scrawled something on what looked like an old paper receipt. He slipped it back to her. It was his phone number.

"I'll be your first contact," Ryan said. "Oh, unless that silly Standard Access saved your contact list. Does that stuff go into the cloud?"

"I dunno," Monica said, even though she was quite sure it did.

Ryan shrugged. "Well, maybe you want a fresh start."

"Because my life's such a failure?"

"What? No. You're many things, but a failure isn't one of them."

"Just a disappointment, then." Monica's skin prickled with resentment at the word.

The old man gave her a strange, sad look. "You've never been a disappointment, Monica."

"Right." Monica glanced back at the car's dashboard. Julia was going to be pissed about the extra charges. "I've gotta go. I'm already late to my appointment."

"Alright," said Ryan, stepping back from the curb. "You can call anytime, you know. If you want."

"Sure."

"I really appreciate you stopping by."

Monica nearly told him it was a mistake, but something in her couldn't bear to see the gleam fade from his eyes.

Well, that was strange, Monica thought as the car zipped the other direction, having made certain the destination in the GPS was the cell store.

She didn't think she knew anyone in this part of town, so she didn't think much of it when the car paused at a light. But then—

"Monica?"

Monica jumped in her seat. Peering at her through her still-open window was her former boss, Lana. She was dressed like she was out for a jog, pulling out her earbuds as she stepped closer to the curb.

To Monica's dismay, the car didn't move when the light turned green, or when she pounded furiously on the controls.

"Hey, Lana," she said, hoping her grimace looked at least a bit like a smile.

"What brings you back to town?"

"Just needed a change."

"A change from the change, huh?" Lana laughed. Monica was unamused. She figured Lana was referencing her resignation letter, in which she'd excused her sudden departure with some half-true bull about needing a 'major life change to more closely align herself with her goals'.

It had been almost four years since she'd quit small-town advertising, clawing towards the big city's major agencies but falling short in each of her gigs. Mike had been the one with the finance job, who made enough to buy his own place. Monica had been as much a part of his apartment as the perfectly fine sofa they'd thrown on the curb last summer when he'd decided to get a bigger one.

"It wasn't what I expected," she said honestly, knowing any other excuse would open her up for more invasive questions.

"I know the feeling," Lana said. "I tried it once myself, you know. I was sold on the big city glory. People were always telling me things were better there, I could go higher. Make more money, you know? But after a couple years working my ass off, I realized no one had ever told me I'd be *happier* there. So, I came back."

Monica was surprised; Lana never talked about her time in the city. She couldn't understand how someone could gloss over something like that. Hadn't she felt ashamed, dragging herself back to this sleepy little suburb? Hadn't she felt defeated, like the city had won and spat her out?

"Well, it was good seeing you," Lana said when it became clear Monica was reluctant to chat. "Oh, and if you know anyone who's looking for ad work, we've actually just had a position open up. Tell them to call HR anytime. Ah, here. I know people don't do paper anymore, but we just got some new cards." Lana dug in her fanny pack and beamed as she handed Monica a business card.

"Thanks," Monica said as the car started up again of its own accord. "I'll think about it."

After she'd rounded the corner, Monica made the car pull over. She prodded the dashboard, trying to get that first screen to reappear. "Manual entry. *Manual entry!*"

"Now recalculating route," the car replied.

"No! No recalculating! Let me type the address!"

"Recalculation complete. Now continuing guidance."

"Argh!"

The car dipped back into the flow of traffic, despite Monica's attempts to halt it. Eventually, she gave in; at least the cell store icon was displayed up ahead. Then the car stopped, this time for construction traffic.

"Oh, come on!" she shouted. With the new system, traffic was meant to be a relic of the past. She'd had enough of the past for one day.

Then she glanced out the window, and immediately wanted to bury her head in her hands.

Staring back at her from the next car over was Nate, her previous ex.

Monica let out a defeated sigh. She couldn't pretend she hadn't seen him. Not when the traffic was deadlocked, and both of their windows were open.

"Hey, Nate," she said after an awkward pause.

"Hey, Nicky."

"I didn't know you were still living here."

"I didn't know you were back."

"I'm not back. I'm just… recalibrating."

Nate arched an eyebrow. "The big city wasn't everything you thought it'd be?"

Better than being stuck in a tiny shithole, she wanted to retort. It was probably what he expected her to say. After all, they'd ended things when she'd called his desire to build a life here 'the fantasy of failure'. Because she was going to do so much better without him, right? Four years later, she'd sure shown him.

Her throat tightened. "No. It wasn't."

Nate frowned. "Did something happen?"

"No, it was just…" Monica glanced away, but no matter where she looked, she couldn't find the words.

"It just wasn't for you?" Nate finished for her.

Monica shook her head. "It doesn't matter. I'm moving on."

Nate searched her expression for a moment, then shrugged. "Alright. Hope things work out for you."

Monica stared. That was it? He'd been right, in the end. She'd been wrong. Didn't he want to make that clear to her? Didn't he want to gloat?

The traffic still wasn't moving. She couldn't even see what was causing it up ahead. Now they were stuck here in an awkward silence, her cheeks burning like she had a fever. Why was everyone being so nice to her, as if they'd forgotten all the horrible things she'd said and done? Did she really look that pathetic?

How could Julia not be judgmental, her father not disappointed, her former boss not indifferent, her old ex not smug?

Wasn't that how they'd been before?

That was how she would have felt.

She looked at the dashboard. The Moirai logo danced ambiently on the GPS screen, the car in its 'resting' state until the deadlock broke. The route was still pointing towards the cell store, despite the detour. But Monica was starting to gather that this wasn't the only thing it had pulled from her data.

If it was trying to embarrass her, it had succeeded. She really had nothing left to lose.

"Nate, wait," she said, even though neither of their cars were moving. "I'm… sorry, for the things I said. About your dreams, about this town. We had different goals, and I didn't understand that. I hope you've had better luck with yours than I have with mine."

Nate looked surprised. "I dunno about luck. Things have been up and down since then. But now I'm just taking it as is comes. Every problem has its place and time, right? It's like these cars— you can try to map your route as much as you'd like, but sometimes you just hit construction that isn't in the system. You could get out and pick a fight with the builder-bots, or you can just relax and wait for it to clear."

"That's very Zen of you."

Nate shrugged. "Makes things easier to manage, I guess. Or maybe it just makes them less disappointing."

After years of imagining his life had improved meteorically after their breakup, Monica was stunned. But before she could respond, the line of cars ahead began to move.

"Ah, looks like we're free," he said. "Look, if you need someone to talk to, you can give me a call anytime. Being stuck in traffic feels a bit less shitty when you know we're all stuck in it together, doesn't it?"

His car pulled ahead, his lane moving faster than hers.

Monica slumped back in her seat as her car proceeded. She'd always thought this town was an eddy, a stagnant cesspool where dreams went to die. Even Lana, the picture of perfect suburbia, had felt the same. Yet something had brought her back and kept her here. It wasn't that she was a brainwashed townie, as Monica always thought— she had sampled another life and decided it wasn't for her.

Maybe she, like Nate, was taking things as they came.

Maybe that was enough.

And maybe that was okay.

She glanced up, hoping to catch Nate's attention, but his car was gone. Of course. It was just her luck. She had always racked up missed opportunities like road miles.

Her car trundled forward. Then it stopped. This time, it was just a light. But—

"Nicky!"

Monica looked. Somehow, she'd pulled alongside Nate again. He was writing something down on a scrap of paper.

"Gimme a goalpost," he said, just like when they were dating. Automatically, Monica shaped it with her fingers. Nate folded the paper into a little ball and flicked it from his car to hers. He scored.

The light turned green.

"I'd forgotten to tell you, I got a new number!" he shouted as his car pulled further ahead. Anything else was lost to the hum of the electric vehicles.

Monica watched him disappear. Then her car began to slow, and she groaned. *Not again.*

But as the car rolled up to the cell store, she let out a sigh of exaltation.

The GPS pinged. "You have arrived at your destination."

That evening, Monica sat in her sister's guest room with her new phone. A blank slate, her memories backed up safely to the cloud.

From her pocket, she withdrew three pieces of paper— a receipt, a business card, and an unfolded football.

Anytime, they had said, and Monica realized they actually might have meant it.

She picked one and dialed.

IF THIS GOES ON DON'T PANIC

ALAN BAILEY
An experienced podcaster, educator and SFF enthusiast

http://itgodp.libsyn.com/
@if_this_goes_on

CAT RAMBO
A Nebula Winning & World Fantasy nominated Fantasy & SF writer/editor/teacher

JOINED BY
Graeme Barber of POCGamer.com & Diane Morrison, host of SFWA's The Panel

Every month we interview SFF writers, editors, activists, and gamers about their experiences with genre fiction and the idea of hope.

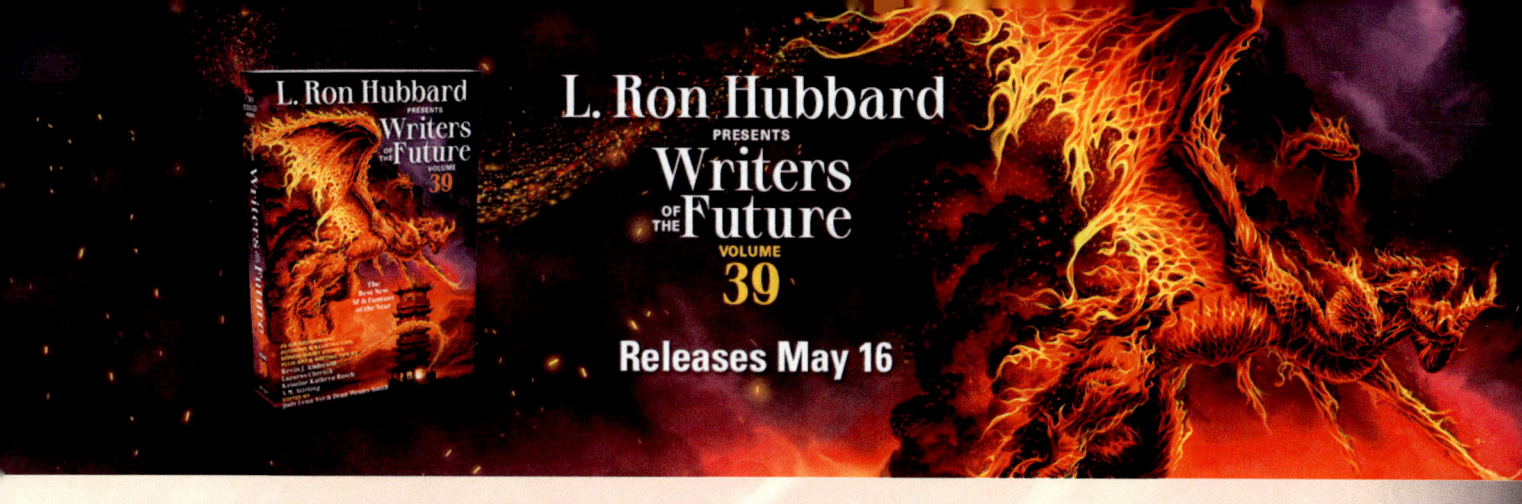

CALLING ALL NEW READERS, WRITERS & ILLUSTRATORS!

IT'S TIME TO DISCOVER
WRITERS OF THE FUTURE VOLUME 39

ROCKETING TO YOU FASTER-THAN-LIGHT FROM THE FUTURE

If you're an aspiring speculative-fiction author, here's your latest how-to manual.

If you're already a die-hard fan, then this issue needs no introduction.

Are you ready for the May launch?

With unforgettable stories ranging from aliens in your TV set, to shapeshifters; from challenging your concept of how to decide what's real, to regaining your innate powers; and immortal tips from the great Masters, you're sure to be entertained and expanded.

All you have to do is turn the page and enter your own private multiverse of pure imagination. So grab a cup o' joe and let's whet your appetite.

Tips from the Tops:

"Every year the Writers of the Future Contest inspires new writers and helps to launch their careers. The combination of reward, recognition, instruction, and opportunity for beginning authors is unparalleled. There is no contest comparable to the Writers of the Future."

—*Rebecca Moesta Writers of the Future Contest judge*

In every issue, you'll find the wisdom of contest founder, L. Ron Hubbard. Here are his thoughts about the power of science fiction to change the world.

"Science fiction does NOT come after the fact of a scientific discovery or development. It is the herald of possibility. It is the plea that someone should work on the future. Yet it is not prophecy. It is the dream that precedes the dawn when the inventor or scientist awakens and goes to his books or his lab saying, 'I wonder whether I could make that dream come true in the world of real science.' …

"You have satellites out there, man has walked on the moon, you have probes going to the planets, don't you? Somebody had to dream the dream, and a lot of somebodies like those great writers of The Golden Age and later had to get an awful lot of people interested in it to make it true."

—*L. Ron Hubbard Battlefield Earth, Introduction*

This genre provides a powerful platform to "Write the Future You Want to Live In." Just look around at the giant leaps forward in technology, many of which were inspired by science fiction over the last century. You too can influence positive change!

Welcome to the largest forum on planet Earth for inciting interest in speculative fiction!

Tips from WOTF Podcast 44: Writing Short Stories that Sell, from Contest Judges

"Have a purpose for your story, know where you're going with it, and don't go off on tangents because you don't have the real estate to do that [in a short story]. You need to keep in mind what your story is, what your character's goal is and go there! Of course, don't forget your twist at the end."

—*Jodi Lynn Nye, Contest Coordinating Judge*

Ready for story teasers? Here we go!

Masterful Art and Writing Tips:

"Circulate" by L. Ron Hubbard: Do you ever wish for an effective formula, the cure for writer's block?

"What Is Art Direction?" by Lazarus Chernik: How can artists realize their dream in the fast world of marketing?

"Prioritize to Increase Your Writing" by Kristine Kathryn Rusch: What does it mean for a creative person to take care of yourself?

Bonus Short Stories:

"Fire in the Hole" by Kevin J. Anderson: Dan Shamble, Zombie P.I., 'nuff said!

"The Unwilling Hero" by L. Ron Hubbard: What would you do if your editor ordered you to outer space?

"Constant Never" by S. M. Stirling: Knights and dragons, unexpectedly perverse.

12 Award-Winning Authors—Story Synopses

"Kitsune" by Devon Bohm: A miracle? An omen? Or something else? One day, they arrived in droves—the foxes of the desert, the field, the imagination. …

"Moonlight and Funk" by Marianne Xenos: When a vampire, a dragon and a shape-shifting Chihuahua meet on a beach in Key West, fireworks go off! But that's just the background. "Moonlight and Funk" by Marianne Xenos

"Death and the Taxman" by David Hankins: The Grim Reaper, trapped in an IRS agent's dying body, must regain his powers before he dies and faces judgment for his original sin.

"Under My Cypresses" by Jason Palmatier: In a metaverse future, a woman who exposes falseness in others must decide what is real to her—the love she lost or the love she may have found.

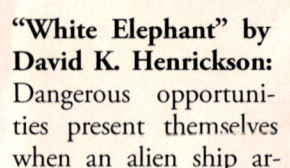

"White Elephant" by David K. Henrickson: Dangerous opportunities present themselves when an alien ship arrives in the solar system seeking repairs.

"Piracy for Beginners" by J. R. Johnson: With her spaceship at the wrong end of a pirate's guns, a former war hero must face down her enemies and demons to save Earth's last best chance for peace.

"A Trickle in History" by Elaine Midcoh: Years after the Second Holocaust, the last surviving Jews on earth attempt to rewrite the past.

"The Withering Sky" by Arthur H. Manners: When I said I'd do anything to pay off my debts and get back home to Earth, I didn't mean survey a derelict spaceship at the edge of the solar system—but here I am.

"The Fall of Crodendra M." by T. J. Knight: High-powered telescopes bring galactic life to our TVs, and network tuner Hank Enos figures he's seen everything—until the day an alien boy stares back.

"The Children of Desolation" by Spencer Sekulin: Determined to save his wife, Tumelo takes an unlikely client through South Africa's ruins to the heart of the Desolation—a journey that will cost or save everything.

"Timelines and Bloodlines" by L. H. Davis: When a terrorist smuggles a nuclear weapon into London, a team regresses in time to AD 1093 to assassinate a knight on the battlefield, thereby eliminating the terrorist a millennia before his birth.

"The Last History" by Samuel Parr: The Grand Exam, a gateway to power for one, likely death for all others—its entrants include ambitious nobles, desperate peasants, and Quiet Gate, an old woman with nothing left to lose.

Early Accolades! The International Review of Book's Badge of Achievement:

Herein follow juicy excerpts:

Well done! No corner of the speculative fiction genre has been left untouched with these epic stories told by the hottest new authors and illustrated by the most talented within the industry.

Winning a spot in the Writers of the Future Contest is a serious career-making event for writers and illustrators, many of whom send in submissions for years. Upon winning they are ferried off to Hollywood to revel in their new fame and glory, rubbing shoulders with the greats of the past and present in a glittering lights and black-tied affair. They are chosen for their freshness and skill, offering the judges their rare stories and gifted illustrations.

The book was transcendent, and as my only focus should be on recommending it to fellow readers, that I can do with heart and soul, and argue that the worlds to which the stories teleport their readers are far more special and grand than a black tie event in Hollywood.

The true winners in the Writers of the Future Contest? Readers!

These stunningly talented authors and illustrators can have their well-deserved fame, and I will remain at home greedily devouring their stories a second time, and perhaps a third. The beauty of this compilation of short stories is the pure pleasure in the myriad writing styles, voices, characters, and worlds. Each story is completely different from all those that came before and after.

So for speculative fiction readers everywhere, this book represents the best and brightest upcoming authors and illustrators within the genre, and with this breakout introduction to their work, you'll one day be able to brag that you were their devoted fans from the beginning.

I Want to Enter the Contest! What Do I Do?

Good for you! It takes courage to step forth, esteemed warrior!

First, you'll want to peruse the anthology itself, to assess the market and get a feel for today's standard in speculative fiction. Of course, also for fun while thinking outside the box.

Next, look over the contest guidelines to be sure you qualify as an amateur writer.

Then, write the story that's inside you! Perhaps something about that future you want to live in…

Personally, I felt thrilled to receive the Semi-Finalist Award the first time I entered a few years ago. It represented the validation I needed from top professional science-fiction authors, to keep on going! I also revere the handwritten note I received from top judge Dave Farland on my strengths and how to improve further. When I need inspiration, I remember his opening words, "I read every line of your story with great interest."

Many who enter the contest regularly, say that the quarterly deadline gives them a calendar target to shoot for. Not to mention the carrot on the stick—a chance for attendance at a high-profile one-week workshop given in Hollywood by industry leaders on craft and marketing.

And all culminating with the annual Gala event to match up illustrators with authors, announce the winners on-stage, and marvel as the crowd lines up for your book signing!

Winners have gone on to grace the pages of New York Times bestseller lists; while illustrators have contributed to movies, comic books, and album covers.

Let's get writing; and see you there!

By Dr. Lee Carroll

About the Author
Dr. Lee Carroll

Working abroad in 10 countries of Europe, Asia, Africa, North and South America, both as a doctor and teacher, has shown me life as a prism of viewpoints. That experience has enriched my writing, to the point where I enjoy showcasing the admiration I feel for varied cultures. For example, my WOTF Semi-finalist entry is published for Kindle as Death Clearinghouse: The Novelette [B07TM3X2RY], featuring Apache ingenuity. When I'm not writing, I'm yanking swords out of stones around the world. Amazon author page: https://www.amazon.com/stores/author/B07TRC1F4V/about)

THE Park
By Teresa Milbrodt

The problem is lot rent. Unless you live in a mobile home park, you probably don't realize that you can own a home but not the land it's on. Everyone who lives in Shady Forest Estates (which has neither shade nor a forest) is walking a financial tightrope, living on a fixed income or minimum wage. Lot rents have been increasing, which poses a difficulty unless your house can levitate. Mine have been able to do so in the past but it's not an option for everyone, like my neighbors, Pat and Emma, who come for coffee every other day.

I appreciate the familiarity, how they hug me, kiss both cheeks, and bring some form of baked good. They've lived in Shady Forest for twenty years, since Pat became a widow, Emma got divorced, and the sisters bought a trailer together. Pat worked in an elementary school cafeteria for years and decorates cakes to order. Emma works three days a week at the fabric store and doesn't know how long she can keep it up with the arthritis in her knees, but now she and Pat are fretting over the two newest families in the park.

"They have troubles," says Pat. "Financial troubles." She, Emma, and I have taken a liking to the children who we see playing in the front yards. Shady Forest isn't bad— we have summer picnics, a Halloween haunted pasture, and too many holiday decorations, but the park was purchased a few years ago by a new company. That's when the problems started, you understand, now that our landlords are faceless entities who consider us only as rent checks.

I don't explain the jars of herbs in my kitchen, but folks have learned that I know everything their grandmas did and a pinch more. I tell everyone that I'm from Oregon— mostly true since I moved there years ago and found a secluded glen where I could perch my cottage. I came to Shady Forest since I needed a place that was more peopled, a place where I could find new heroes.

Sometimes I miss the old days and my fence of shining bones graced with the skulls that welcomed me home. Too many brash young people visited my forest cottage, and some of their heads were destined to decorate my abode. My heroes were more fleeting. I never saw them after they completed their mission to save their beloved from a giant, or steal their sibling's heart back from some other witch. I was fine with fleeting relationships, assumed their happily-ever-after and waited for the next worthy person to emerge from the forest, requiring a magical knife or comb or doll.

Now my heroes have smaller but more persistent needs. They are older women who want tea, a chat, and a knowing nod. The dark-haired maidens have become grandmothers, their salt-and-pepper tresses bound in a kerchief, women who worry over grown children, fret over grandkids they are raising, or ache quietly for spouses who have passed on. They don't believe in therapists. They believe in tea. Tea doesn't purport to fix anything, but sometimes it does.

Four afternoons a week I work at the Adult Education Center as a GED tutor. Most of the tutors are older folks, retired teachers. Our students are in their twenties and sometimes their thirties, balancing jobs, children, and silver-edged dreams.

"I've been snippy at home," Lydia admits. "Have to drop the kids at Mom's place for a bit so I can breathe and have study time." After work she's bleary-eyed and frazzled, makes dinner then drives here to cram a mountain of figures into her mind. Like most of my neighbors she lurches from paycheck to paycheck. Sometimes we work until the yawning hours of the night, but it's easier to occupy myself here rather than wonder what to do when the moon is full and I recall old hungers.

You might be curious how I control those urges, but children are no longer a strong culinary temptation. There are times, however, when I hear them argue or tease each other outside my cottage and I feel a certain twinge. My role as she-who-is-to-be-feared is rather ingrained, even when I think I have abandon such habits.

When Emma cares for her grandchildren on the weekend, Pat visits me to lament. You can imagine that sisters always have an opinion on each other's doings.

"She's a sweetheart and a softy," says Pat. "Emma gives her daughter whatever extra money she has after groceries and rent, then she's babysitting. Doesn't have a life of her own."

"It's what she thinks a grandma should do," I say. "Do you think she doesn't want to help her daughter as much as she does?"

"She wants to do it, and then complains to me," says Pat. "Why can't Sonia save more money? Why can't she get a babysitter? Then she drives back over there the next weekend."

This is the hero's paradox— the need to feel needed, and simultaneous resentment. I don't know if those valiant grandmas would know what do with themselves if not sacrifice. They were taught to shape their lives around helping others.

"If I go out with friends, I wonder what my grandkids are doing," says Emma. "I figure Sonia found an inexperienced babysitter and she's feeding my grandbabies junk." Heroic grandmas don't know anything but the hero's quest, saving people over and over.

The single working mother is another type of hero. Lydia has many stories of trying to arrange weekend visits with the kids' dad —it's part of the custody agreement— but she drops them off at his mom's place instead.

"They miss their dad even if they don't say so," she says. "Why did I marry such an ogre?" Another question that has no response, but love can be so bright that it's difficult to see past the glare.

My next-door neighbor Russell doesn't imagine himself to be a gray-haired prince, but he shyly invites me for coffee.

"I bought a box of vanilla wafers and I don't eat them fast enough," he says in way of explanation. How can I not be amused? His hands are large and wrinkled with clean fingernails. He checks once, twice, to make sure I have enough sugar and cream for my coffee, then asks about my students at the Adult Education Center.

"My wife was a teacher," he offers. Russell wants the comfort of another body beside him on the couch and in bed at night, another pair of slippers shuffling around the kitchen. He imagines he's older than me, but I appear static in age, gaunt with long gray hair pulled back in a smart bun. I smile with my mouth closed to hide my sharp teeth. Russell sparks with loneliness that would beautify any face.

On Friday evening he asks if I would like to watch a movie. I sit with him on the couch, amused at his little glances and the way he rubs his hands together. His ghost wife sits on his other side and gives me a solemn smile. After the movie I let him kiss my cheek, say this has been lovely and I must be going. I don't expect his tears, but he tries to brush them away.

"I'm sorry," he says. "This happens when I'm tired."

His ghost wife pats his shoulder. I pat his other shoulder and say it's okay, the night hours are strange. I pad back to my cottage and tell myself I am not shaken. I've never lived beside people who carry so much sadness and worry in backpacks and tote bags, unable to rest their loads.

When I linger on Pat and Emma's porch during a long evening chat, we hear the fights of reasonable people arguing over the last five dollars in the checkbook. We share glances and wonder how many more times the lot rent will be raised. I was accustomed to dealing with various demons and devils in the old country, but not of the financial variety.

Emma and Pat host a neighborhood meeting in their living room and kitchen, cram the double-wide with chairs and pass around cookies to plot what we might do about future rent hikes. The solutions are varied:

Buy lotto tickets.

Have weekly bake sales.

Declare the park a historic site since Woodrow Wilson's grand-niece by marriage used to live here.

I ponder our adversaries, the board of faceless executives who raise the numbers on our monthly bills, and I remember the story of the demon and the young farmer. He had the (mis)fortune of meeting a devil in the forest, one who told him there was a bag of gold buried six feet under a certain tree. The farmer only had to dig a hole and retrieve it. He dug the hole, then crawled out and leaned way over to search for the gold. The demon gave him a shove, and the farmer fell in and broke his neck. If only I could save us by calling forth demons to help executives dig holes, but that feels as futile as a plate of peanut butter cookies. What magic could dissolve the system?

When the serfs rebelled, sometimes there was change but always blood. Mostly theirs.

Russell sits beside me, his hand over mine, and asks if I'd like another cookie.

"It's like they want to force us all out," Pat mutters. "But our houses can't fly." Even if their homes were like mine and could sprout chicken legs, where could we walk them to under the glistening stars? My usual forms of remedy and revenge are not effective here. It would be a fine thing to see those corporate heads lined up on my fence posts so I could give them a talking-to, as in days past. Most of the skulls I collected were obstinate at first, but after a few years they came around. I assume my neighbors would be dismayed if I rebuilt my fence of bones, no matter whose skulls graced them. I cannot conjure against capitalism.

When Lydia is too rattled to focus on her studies, we pause for coffee as she pours out another story about her ex. He didn't take the kids for the weekend since he was going on a trip with friends.

"He doesn't care if he wrings their hearts out," she says. "Then he's late on child support, and I go to the food pantry and ask my mom for another loan. When we got married, he said 'two incomes, two kids, we'll be fine.'"

Lydia is a nursing home attendant, spends long hours helping people get in and out of bed and washing their delicate skin. She wants to be a registered nurse.

"All this school ahead of me feels like climbing Mount Everest," she says. "I'm at the bottom wearing shorts and a t-shirt."

She sips her coffee, opens the math book, sighs.

I didn't expect my students and neighbors to give me stories willingly, different from my previous heroes who I didn't really know at all. They completed a near-impossible task, so I'd grant them magical objects. I gave them the objects, and they tromped away from my cottage as the skulls chattered good-bye. I don't remember them as teary and needing hugs. I didn't imagine my frail self could comfort someone in that way.

In the old days my heroes married their true loves. Lydia says it's easier to go it alone and trade babysitting duties with friends.

"Mom is still mad about the divorce," she says, "but we were so young when we got married, and he never shaped up. Now I feel like a bad parent. My kids eat too much macaroni and cheese and peanut butter."

"You're doing the best you can," I say.

"I'm never home," she says. "They'll forget what I look like."

Lydia isn't fighting giants but filling in bubbles to the tick of a clock. I doubt my past and present heroes would switch places. The dragon you know is better than the dragon you don't. Quests take different forms, as do rewards and villains, but the struggle doesn't end. In lieu of enchanted mirrors and combs, I offer more coffee.

I don't know why I'm drawn to the law library, but it's a block away from the Adult Education Center and one afternoon I decide to peruse local zoning and building ordinances. Perhaps I'm enamored with the idea of paperwork spells, and the books of incantations I no longer use have given me the stamina to withstand legal language. Those hexes and charms had so many contradictions, clauses, and times when they should and should not be performed. The labyrinth of local ordinances does not seem dissimilar, and it has a power I did not contend with in a land ruled by feudal lords.

I realize how silly my plan to combat leases with laws may be, but I have no other solution. I recruit Russell and Pat to help scan the seas of text, trying to disregard my fear of failure. In my old life I knew my role by rote, so this is rather unsettling.

"There's no law too strange to ignore," I say to Russell and Pat. "The older the better. People forgot them long ago."

"Like us," says Pat.

She and Russell get eyestrain after a couple hours and ask if we can break for coffee. Pages after pages of tiny type have left them discouraged. I rub Russell's shoulder with my thin fingers and say of course they should get coffee. I'll stay a bit longer.

"How do you have the energy?" says Russell with a smile of envy or admiration.

"I work best in the evenings," I say. Mine is a world of excuses. We continue our work after they return, but I don't realize how long we've read until Pat and Russell yawn and glance sideways like they're suspicious of my stamina. Perhaps that is my own worry. I never had to cultivate relationships, you understand, and don't want people to think me too strange. I pretend to weary and say yes, enough for today, we should find something to eat.

My hero, my Lydia, passes the GED after two months of bleary-eyed training. She appears at the Adult Education Center with a smile of triumph and fatigue, waving her white paper like a flag. Now she must organize her application materials for community college.

"I made it over the foothills," she says, slumping against me in a way that no hero ever did, but I've come to expect this casual embrace of exhaustion.

"Coffee first," I say, "and then forms."

Lydia grants me a tired nod and squeezes my hand. My old bones are still surprised by touch, but it is another result of having heroes who don't fade into the forest.

I've nearly exhausted my wisps of hope when Russell finds an ordinance related to the upkeep of historic structures. Such homes must have controlled rent policies if the tenants are responsible for maintaining the buildings in good repair.

"I bet it was designed to keep those Victorian houses on Main Street looking good," says Pat. "Shady Forest has a bunch of homes that are over fifty years old. You don't find them everywhere, especially that queer little cottage of yours. I don't recall how you moved it to the lot. Is it over fifty years old?"

"A few years past," I say.

We copy the documents and crowd Pat and Emma's kitchen when Emma's granddaughter visits —a sweet young woman who just received her law degree— and whose eyes spark at the chance to have her own court battle while working as a paralegal. We can't pay more than pocket change and cookies, but she grins.

"My law school friends will have ideas," she says. "We may not win, but we can tie things up for a while. Nothing like a fly in the ointment."

We only need another month, another month, another month of stable rent until those dismal corporate dragons decide we're not worth the trouble. We never truly vanquish the villains, they just appear in different forms, a shifting battle of serfs versus lords in different times and places, heroes wielding swords and sticks and statutes as we dig our toes deeper into the dirt.

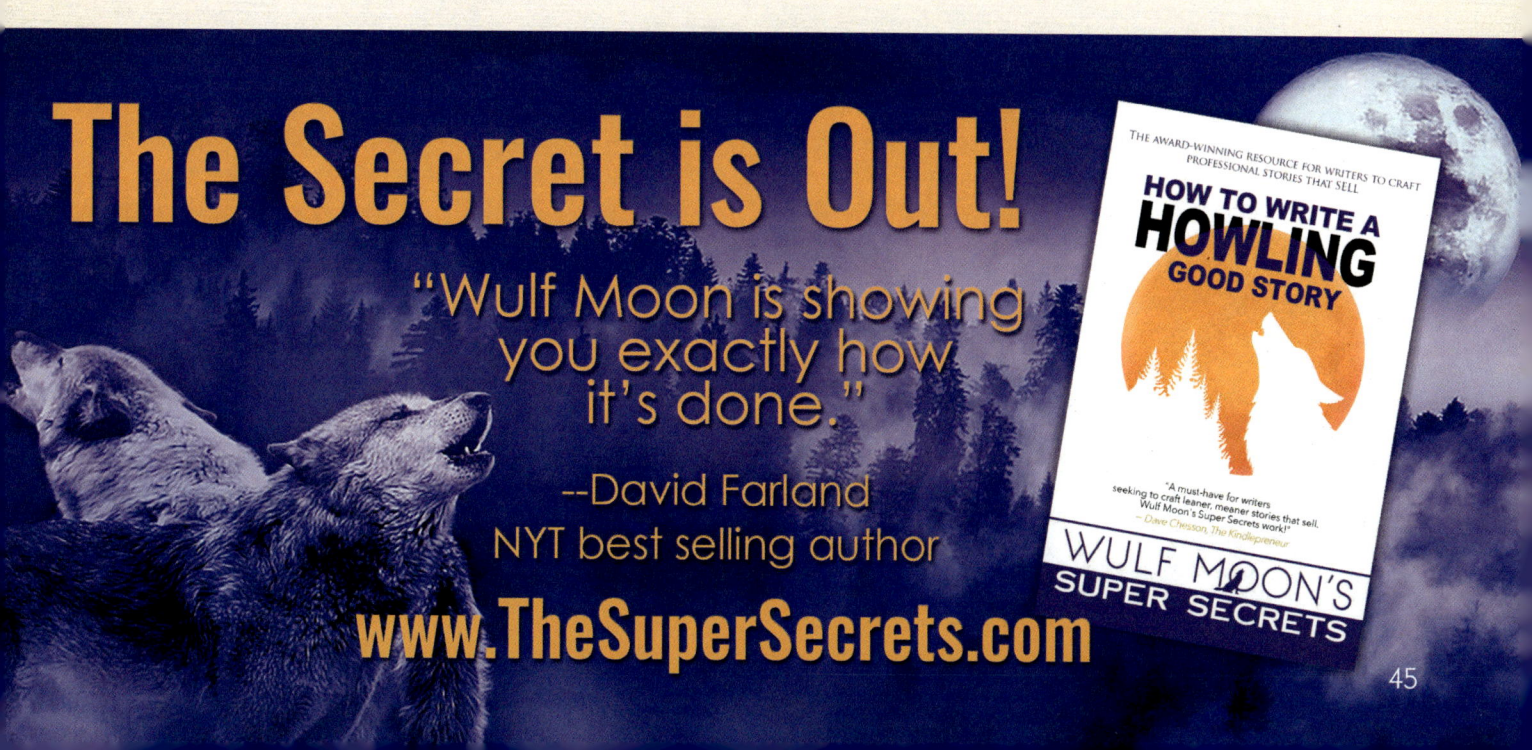

A Language Older Than Words

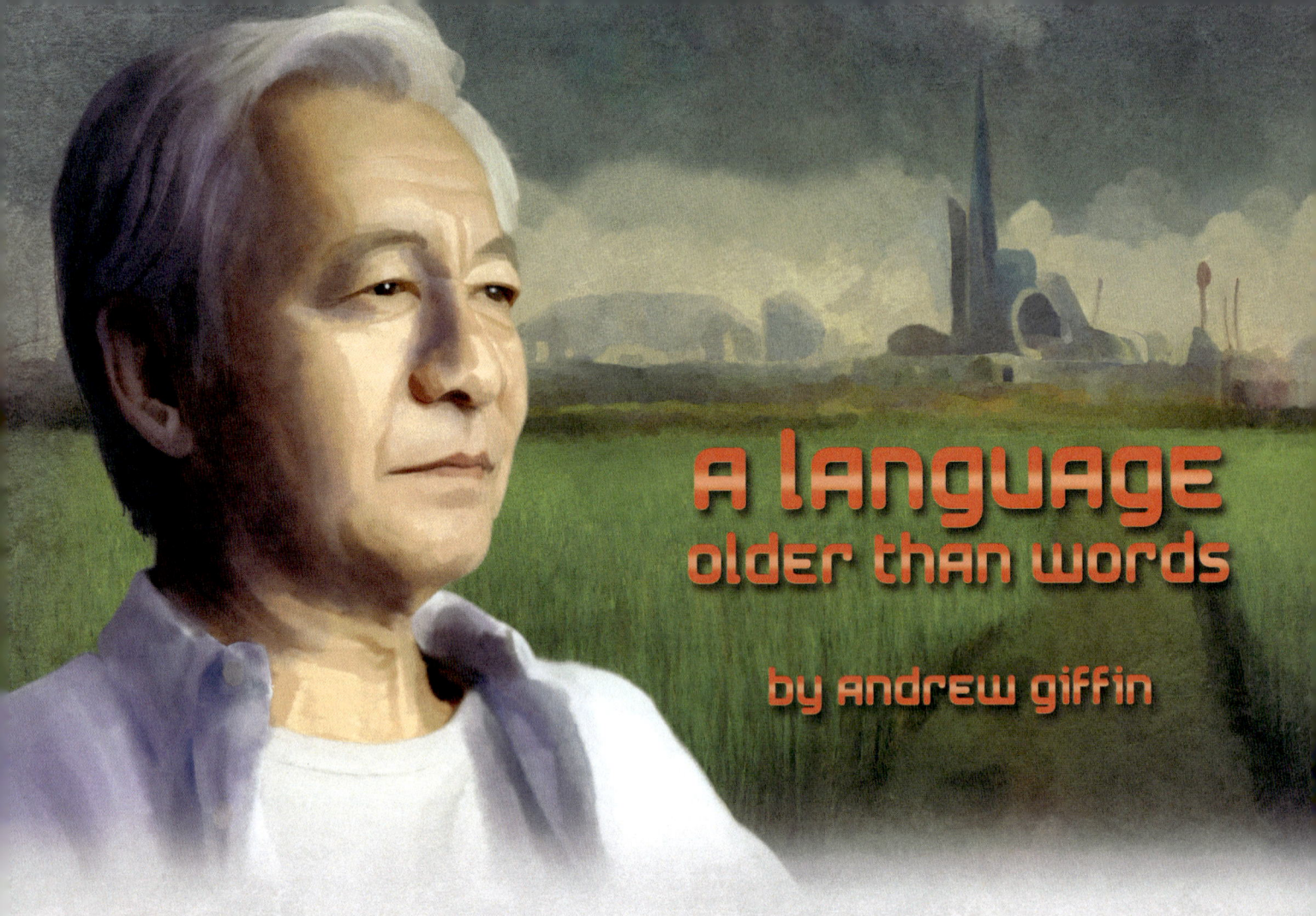

by Andrew Giffin

Hotaka Tanaka dreamed again of his first sushi from Earth. The tuna tasted so clean. It almost melted, absorbed by the rice as the wasabi warmed his tongue. The eel nigiri was light with a hint of sweetness, the sauce dark and smoky.

The delivery had taken months to arrange. He hired the cheapest courier on the service board, unthinkable to him now. He hated imagining what the fish experienced making planetfall from the station.

But he'd been young. Young and in love. He still managed to propose to Aiko that night, even as his mind reeled from the taste. She said yes.

The sushi dream faded. Though she was dead, he could still feel the weight of Aiko lying next to him, the incline of the bed as her body pressed against it. A sliver of skin on her lower back would show where her shirt shifted in the night, the softness of her hair spreading across her pillow to graze his arm.

He opened his eyes to confirm he was alone. With a groan, he sat up and put his aching feet on the cold floor. His reflection showed an old man in a robe blinking sleep from his eyes. He turned away, his wedding ring catching the morning light as he kissed his fingers and pressed them to Aiko's pillow.

He passed through the house, to his backyard and the rice paddies. Aiko walked her biology students down the rows of crops as they took notes, a field trip. Hotaka blinked the memory away and stepped outside.

A light drizzle fell as the automated harvesters moved through the rice, leaving behind a trail of slashed stalks. The paddy drained itself into automated trenches in the night, the water bound for the treatment plant.

He arrived at a series of tanks near the harvester garage. Hotaka had partially subsidized to afford the tanks, despite his grandfather having bought out their shares from the collective. Theirs was the first colony farm to go private; thankfully his father passed before Hotaka's first subsidy. He never had the heart to tell him his true passion lived in these tanks.

He climbed the wooden steps and lifted the lid, revealing the carp inside. They swam in the seaweed, feeding on the crabs crawling along the bottom of the tanks amongst clams and mussels. Aiko stood next to him, watching a carp as it darted from one corner of the tank to the other. She drew sketches in her notebook, except she wasn't really there.

Hotaka took a bucket of water and net from the side of the tank and scooped the fish out. It flopped in the air as its gills searched for water, and he dropped it in the bucket.

Aiko explained the ecosystem inside the tank to her students. "The carp eat the crabs, the crabs eat the seaweed, and the mussels help filter the water. Four different species, working together to form a stable ecosystem. The same spirit of cooperation that brought us here, to this system, this world."

One of her students raised a hand. "Weren't the original settlers forced laborers? Before the revolution?"

Aiko nodded. "Yes, that's true. Although it's important never to forget, the cooperation that built our collective is only possible because of forgiveness." She looked into Hotaka's eyes. "Forgiveness built a better world." He replaced the lid and climbed back down with the fish.

The memories evaporated as he stopped short at his porch. Wet footprints traveled across the wood towards the open back door of his house. He'd closed the door. Now it stood open.

He approached with curiosity instead of fear, unlike the night Aiko had been killed. What else could be taken from him now?

He stepped into his house and could see nothing disturbed. Water was running in the kitchen. A man stood at the sink, washing his face and hands. He lifted his shirt, splashing water under his arms.

Hotaka retained a sense of calm. He put the fish on the kitchen table, and the man looked up at last. Their eyes met, and the man took a few quick steps backwards, startled.

The man wasn't Japanese. He had short, black hair and light brown skin, his chin peppered with a few day's stubble. He appeared to be in his early forties. The lower right corner of his shirt was bloody.

"Hello," Hotaka said in Japanese, the language of the colony.

The man blinked and said something in a language he didn't recognize.

"What are you doing in my house?" Hotaka moved closer.

The man took another step back and bumped into the kitchen counter. His face was frightened, as if he were the homeowner and Hotaka the intruder.

Hotaka held up his hands to show him there was nothing to fear. "Do you speak Japanese?"

Again the man didn't respond.

He put a hand on his chest. "Tanaka-san," he said, tapping his collarbone for emphasis.

The man tapped on his own chest. "Juan."

Hotaka nodded. Everyone in the colony spoke Japanese, so he'd never needed a translation app. He pulled up his wristpad. With the colony's low-speed connection, the app would take ninety minutes to download. He shrugged and made the purchase before pointing to the blood on the man's clothing. "Are you hurt? Do you need help?" He walked around the kitchen counter.

Juan again stepped away, and for the first time Hotaka noticed the gun sticking out of the waist of the man's pants.

Aiko's body, torn apart by the exit wound, blinked in and out of existence on the floor between them. This wasn't the man who murdered her. He was dead. They'd caught and executed him.

But Hotaka couldn't help feeling this was the same person, returned to finish the job. Or maybe they were both possessed by the same murderous spirit. His lips peeled back in a snarl, his muscles tensed, his heart racing.

Andrew Giffen

"You son-of-a-bitch, that's not your blood. You killed someone with that gun, didn't you? Didn't you!" His voice rose in intensity, shouting the last few words. Juan's eyes widened, glancing towards the open back door.

Aiko leaned over to whisper in his ear. "I wonder what kind of murderer eyes the exit instead of killing an old man who blocks his escape?"

He took a step and shoved Juan with one hand, surprising himself. Juan raised both hands in protest, letting himself be shoved. He was much younger than Hotaka and could easily overtake him, especially with the gun.

Aiko's voice returned, telling him he should try communicating. Instead Hotaka found himself emboldened by the combination of Juan's passivity and their inability to understand each other, unleashing twenty-three years' worth of grief and helplessness and anger.

Adrenaline flooded Hotaka's veins, strengthening his stiff joints as he battered him with closed fists. Juan shielded himself with his hands, crouching down to make himself a smaller target. Hotaka grabbed a glass, throwing it at his head. Juan ducked, and it shattered against the counter behind him. Hotaka was cursing now, yelling a string of obscenities he was surprised he knew.

Juan lunged past him, attempting to flee before slipping on his own wet footprint. He crashed to the ground, the gun sliding across the floor. Hotaka and Juan blinked at the weapon before both lunging after it.

Hotaka was closer. He stood with it pointed at Juan, his first time holding a gun. It was heavier than he expected. Juan froze.

"Get up," Hotaka said. When Juan didn't move, he remembered the man didn't speak Japanese and motioned with the gun for him to stand. Juan scrambled to his feet.

"How dare you come into my house. How dare you take the life of another. You're scum. You aren't worth the air you breathe. I should kill you right now. Nothing would happen to me if I did. They'd call it self-defense, and no one would care what happened to you. You son-of-a-bitch. How dare you take Aiko from me." These words poured from Hotaka, like water rushing from a collapsed dam.

He kept the gun trained on Juan. The man muttered under his breath, his hands folded together as if in prayer.

Hotaka hesitated. Juan didn't act how he expected a murderer to act. He pictured a shadow stalking the streets and searching for blood, a vampire from a silent film. This was the second murderer he'd met in his life, and neither matched up with this image.

The man who killed Aiko had been fleeing a robbery, trying to hide until he could sneak aboard an outgoing transport. Hotaka had been at the spaceport, waiting for his shipment of mussels. Aiko had been sick, running a slight fever and vomiting. Nothing serious, but he still felt guilty for leaving her. She insisted, though. She said she wanted to get some rest, and besides, she wanted some fresh mussel rolls when she woke up.

The murderer later testified he didn't mean to kill her. She'd come into the room behind him. He thought no one was home, pulling the trigger when startled. When he saw what he'd done, he immediately called for an ambulance. It passed Hotaka on his way home, and he could still see the flashing lights in his memory.

At the trial, when his lawyer asked if there was anything else he wanted to say, the man looked Hotaka in the eye and said "I'm sorry." Hotaka had spit before getting up to leave.

He didn't return to hear the guilty verdict. Now Juan stood in his kitchen, looking pathetic as he cowered and prayed.

He lowered the gun and sighed. Juan lifted his head. A light flashed on the side of the grip, and Hotaka inspected the weapon. A message waited on the read-out screen.

"Warning, unauthorized user detected. Weapon will not fire until fingerprint identification with user Haru Sasaki." A picture of Sasaki-san flashed beside the words.

Hotaka looked up. "This isn't your gun, is it?" He pointed it at the floor and squeezed the trigger. Nothing happened. He offered the gun to Juan, who hesitated before taking it. "Try to fire," he instructed, miming the trigger.

Juan nodded, pointing the gun at the floor like Hotaka. He squeezed the trigger. Again, nothing happened. The two men stared at each other.

The forgotten bucket still sat on the kitchen table. Juan glanced over and his stomach growled audibly. Hotaka sighed and pulled a chair out, offering it to him. The man sat slowly, eying him as if he might erupt again.

"Wait here." He grabbed the bucket and walked outside to the harvester garage. At a sink, he killed the fish with a brain spike using the traditional ikejime method. After draining the blood and cutting the spinal cord, he dropped the fish in a slurry of ice water.

He put a carp that had aged for two weeks on a tray as Aiko swept the floor of the garage, singing softly to herself. When he glanced up to watch, she disappeared.

He'd been so proud to make sushi for her once their supply was up and running. "My Hotaka, he brings the world to me," she'd say, smiling as he put the plate in front of her.

He walked back to the house. Shining metal towers dotted the horizon, the colony's urban sprawl a visual reminder of the changing times. He still thought of the system's station as the bustling urban center and their colony as the small rural village on the outskirts. Things hadn't been that way since he was a boy.

Juan swept the glass as Hotaka took the tray of fish into the kitchen. The familiar process of making the sushi was a calming ritual. A few minutes later he had two plates.

"I'll get you a change of clothes," he said as Juan shoveled the food into his mouth.

He went to his bedroom, returning with a pair of pants and a t-shirt. "Here." He offered him the clothes.

Juan said something he didn't understand and took them, nodding at Hotaka in thanks before changing. He reached into his pocket and took out a wrinkled picture. Hotaka ate a piece of sushi, his eyebrows raised at the sight of a physical photo.

Juan sat down and handed it to him. The photo showed Juan and a young girl, obviously his daughter. The resemblance was strong.

Juan pointed at the girl. "Isabel," he said between bites of fish. Hotaka listened as Juan said more, pointing at himself and using his hand to mime a rocketship taking off.

Hotaka pointed at Isabel. "Your daughter?" he said, and Juan nodded, the meaning clear. He spoke more, miming himself crouching before turning and holding his hands up, then running and shoving air.

Hotaka ate another piece of sushi and nodded, though he didn't know what the man was trying to communicate.

He must have escaped from a forced labor colony, Hotaka thought. Not all colonies had abolished the practice like theirs had.

Juan trailed off, and they both lifted their heads at the high-pitch buzz of an approaching transport shuttle. The phone rang, and Juan froze. Hotaka motioned for him to move to the kitchen, then swiped to answer the call.

Hotaka jolted as the head of colony security, Goda-san, appeared. "Tanaka-san. Sorry for the sudden notice. Is your yard clear for a security unit to land?"

"Hold on, I'll check. The harvesters are out today. Everything all right?"

Goda-san wore a suit, as usual, light glistening off his shaved head. The holographic image trailed Hotaka as he stepped out to his backyard. "It's nothing major, something we need to check out. I'll explain when we arrive."

Hotaka nodded. The shuttle grew larger in the distance. On his wristpad, he instructed a harvester to return to the garage. "The yard should be clear in a minute. See you soon." He swiped to end the call and went inside to Juan. "Come with me." He motioned for him to follow.

He grabbed Juan's old clothes along with the gun as they walked outside. Hotaka set a quick pace. The harvester rumbled past, and he threw the gun into the straw walkers, hoping to get it stuck in the metallic conveyor.

He led Juan to the fish tanks. One of them had just been cleaned, and he opened the biofilter panel on the side.

"You'll have to crouch down," he said, miming and pointing to the empty chamber where future fish waste would go. Juan nodded and climbed inside.

Once secured, Hotaka handed him his clothes and closed the panel before rotating the tank, pressing it against its neighbor. The security unit was still several minutes away. He returned to the house, waiting for the shuttle to land.

If they discovered Juan, he would be deported back to wherever he escaped from, likely executed. The labor colonies made examples of failed escapes. Hotaka tried not to think about what his own punishment would be as he went to greet them.

Goda-san climbed out of the front passenger seat. Four men climbed out of the back, the pilot remaining inside. They wore helmets with augmented reality visors covering their eyes.

Goda-san shook his hand, yelling over the sound of the shuttle's engines as they powered down. "Tanaka-san, didn't mean to alarm you."

"Not at all."

The men fanned out to the property behind him. They moved in an organized fashion through the muddy fields of rice. Hotaka hoped the tanks would mask Juan on their thermal imagers.

"What's going on?"

"We had a stowaway on one of our delivery shipments, probably trying to reach the station. They found him in the cargo hold during the security sweep. Caught one of my guys by surprise and rushed him. Even stole his gun, for all the good it'll do him with the print lock." Goda-san stood with his hands on his hips, surveying his men as they searched.

"Is your guy okay, the one he attacked?"

"Oh, he's fine. He needed a skin patch on his forehead for a nasty gash when he got knocked over. Otherwise he's fine."

The men reached the end of the paddies. He could hear their chatter over Goda-san's radio. No mention of the tank, but one addressed Goda-san directly. "Sir, Sasaki-san's gun is pinging from inside the garage."

Goda-san picked up his radio. "Anything on the thermals?" Hotaka glanced at the fish tank, his pulse quickening.

"Negative, just the weapon."

He exhaled.

Goda-san turned to him. "You didn't see anything, did you? He was spotted nearby."

Hotaka shook his head. "The only thing out of the ordinary was one of the harvester's jamming up. I recalled it for maintenance." They walked to the garage as Goda-san's men converged ahead of them before the docked harvester.

Andrew Giffen

One of the men reached in and pulled the gun from the straw walker. "It's Sasaki-san's, all right."

Goda-san nodded. "Where was this one when it conked out on you?"

"It was just finishing the south field, on the edge of the property. He must've ditched the gun sometime in the night." Hotaka tried to sound convincing.

Goda-san motioned his men back to the shuttle. Hotaka followed them out of the garage. They approached the fish tanks again, and he tensed as they passed.

"Keep an eye out, will you?" Goda-san said, and Hotaka nodded. The men got back in the shuttle, and the whine of the engine increased in preparation for take off.

"Thanks for your help, Tanaka-san. And save some sushi for me sometime, eh?" He disappeared into the shuttle as it climbed higher and shot across the rice paddies, out of sight.

Hotaka let out a breath and walked to the tanks. He turned the third one around and opened the biofilter panel. Juan blinked in the light. "They're gone, it's safe to come out," he said, indicating with his hand.

Juan stepped out, scanning the sky as if expecting them to return. Hotaka took this as a cue, returning to the house with haste.

Once inside, Juan became visibly more relaxed. Hotaka filled the kettle with water and set it to boil. He paused, then turned and went to the study.

Aiko sat at the computer with a steaming cup of tea as she graded assignments. The room was dark and empty. Hotaka opened Aiko's teaching folder, finding files from her Astronomy course. He called Juan.

Juan appeared, watching curiously as Hotaka projected the local star cluster. Colonized systems glowed green.

"Where's Isabel?" He spread his hand across the map.

Juan examined the display and pointed to a nearby star. Hotaka nodded and made the purchase with his wristpad. The price meant he'd have to sell his remaining shares of the farm back to the collective. At least he'd be able to keep the fish tanks. He could live with that.

He ran a disposable plastic storage drive over his wristpad and handed it to Juan. "They're looking for a stowaway, not someone who can afford commercial transport. Take this and find Isabel." He pointed at the star Juan indicated. "Isabel."

Juan's face softened as he realized what Hotaka had done. "Isabel," he agreed, nodding.

He led Juan to the garage, handing him the keys to a lime green scooter that hadn't been ridden since before Aiko died.

"Just leave it parked at the spaceport, I'll send one of the robots to get it later." He attempted to mime this to Juan.

There's a good chance I'll never see it again. He didn't really care about that. Aiko stood by the scooter, smiling at Hotaka with pride.

"Take care of yourself, Juan." He reached out for a handshake. Juan stared at his extended hand for a moment before bringing him in for a hug instead. He said something, and Hotaka understood the tone but not the words.

They separated, and Hotaka put a hand on Juan's shoulder. He thought of Aiko's lifeless body, and the young man who apologized to him in court.

"I forgive you."

He wiped his eyes with his sleeve as Juan drove the scooter towards the spaceport. A chirp from his wristpad notified him the translation app had finished its download, and he phonetically repeated Juan's final words to him. The app returned, in perfect Japanese, what Hotaka already knew they would be: "Thank you." He deleted the app.

He returned to the kitchen, where his sushi still waited for him. He prepared another plate, setting it in front of an empty chair. Hotaka smiled as he finished his lunch. ⟳

Asylum
By Gretchen Tessmer

we take care of the orphans at our gates

foundling children and changelings mostly
late of rusted iron rails
and so much gritty dust

rat's nest hair and tattooed hands
threadbare jackets and torn teddy bears

tear-stained cheeks
everywhere

I knelt by one of the little ones

(her mud-splashed shoelaces were a tangled mess
that took a proper spell to unravel)

and I asked where she'd come from
just making conversation

she said she'd been on her own
"forever and ever"
            and ever and ever
snatched from her cradle, sold across the sea

then she added, those tears pooling, looking
as downcast as she could be
apologetic even, that she couldn't answer me

"I don't remember where my home is," she mumbled so low

"home is wherever people care about you…" I replied

with a steady timbre, smiling
and with my forefinger, I tipped
her torn teddy's chin right up

(taking needle and thread from my pocket
I'd soon sew him back up)

I promised her fiercely, while licking the string,

"home is here"

THREAD
BY BRET NELSON

As she woke, Edna Perry found herself mid-step, two yards from the bed. She couldn't get enough air. Disasters flooded her mind.

She left her dog behind. It must be dead by now.

She yelled at a client yesterday. She was fired on the spot.

She missed another trial date. The police were on their way.

As her left foot reached the floor, she became aware of her apartment. And she didn't have a dog. And work went well yesterday. And there was no trial. These crises weren't real.

These were night terrors, but she still couldn't get enough air.

Her eyes drifted to the clock. In three hours, she had to be at the client's facility to lead the coven in a tessellation spell.

That wasn't a night terror, that was her job.

She sat on the floor and focused on her breathing. In her memory, Dr. Waring's voice talked through the steps: "Inhale deep into your belly. Exhale through tight lips and make it last four times as long as it took you to inhale. Count your breaths, go slow, be greedy with that air."

So far, she'd only managed to get 55 minutes of sleep tonight. It was too late to take a pill now. It would be stronger than her alarm.

Anchoring herself to the breathing was the only option she had.

●●●●●●

Anthony Finch, the security chief for Thorton-Bryce Freight, did a half-jog across the loading bay toward his assigned station. He was still about twenty paces inside the spell-casting area when Edna called to him. "Mr. Finch, I'd like to get started soon. Are we about ready?"

The half-jog became the best sprint he could manage, juggling his phone, clipboard, and pride. "Yes, sorry, just checking the east doors. You're all good."

"You're good, too. Someday I'm going to convince you to come and work with us, Mr. Finch."

"You've never heard me on karaoke night," he said. "I'm a lousy singer." Laughter rose from the ten people in folding chairs beyond the caution tape. Edna knew all of them, as Thorton-Bryce was a regular client. The coven was on this loading bay at least once a month.

The first few times Spellbound Services did incantations here, the gallery held nearly fifty people. Now, the only Thorton-Bryce employees present were the ones who were required to be there, and most of them were doing other work on their phones and laptops.

Though witchcraft had been legal for decades, industrial partners had only begun hiring magical suppliers about twelve years ago. Hiring openly, that is. Some companies, particularly in eastern Europe, had been quietly using witches for centuries.

This was Edna's sixth year with Spellbound. In that time, she had worked all the way up from assistant to acolyte. Today's incantation had her leading a dozen spell casters. She'd done close to thirty of these tessellation jobs, but on two hours' sleep she was unfocused and overthinking everything.

Edna called out to her group. "Dan? Can you come over here?" Daniel Santiago was contracted last year as part of a diversity program. The national covens were making a lot of noise about hiring men. If smaller concerns, like Spellbound, wanted to compete, they would have to stop discriminating against warlocks as well. So far, the new hires seemed capable.

Dan hustled over, tugging at his robe to keep from tripping. "Yes, Miss Perry?"

"Call me Edna, please. I'm going to step out for a moment. While I'm gone, get a group of four together and do a gauntcast. We need to be sure there's no ink here. Got it?"

"Yes Miss— Edna." As Dan headed back to gather personnel, Edna stepped toward the bathrooms.

Once she got in a stall, she pulled the tortoise-shell pill case from her bag, popped it open, snatched out a tablet, swallowed it dry, snapped the case closed, then returned it to her bag. It was all one move, so well-practiced that she could have done it in front of Dan without him noticing. With the oxycodone on board, she could focus.

The bottle said to take one tablet per day with food. She'd been taking four. That meant juggling two different prescriptions, but one of those just ran out permanently and the other could only be filled every-so-many days. She couldn't get more pills until next week.

Seven pills— five days. She'd have to taper again. That meant one later tonight, two tomorrow, then one a day until Monday. If things got ugly, she could maybe take an extra one, but that meant a day at the end without any pills at all.

Without.

Edna Perry was no stranger to "the taper," having done it several times over the last three years. Tapering was easier than quitting because quitting meant "without."

"Without" was scary as hell.

"Without" meant feeling everything. "Without" meant no more ducking under when a big wave came. Each wave would hit her full force and toss her around and choke her.

What if she quit this time? What if she ran the taper down to zero then stopped taking the pills forever? Would she lose her confidence? Could she talk to a client (or her coven) without stuttering or crying or shutting down? Could she run a job like the one today?

Too dangerous. For now, she was better on the oxy than off it. If that made her an addict then fine, she was an addict.

"Without" was a problem for later.

✦ ✦ ✦ ✦ ✦ ✦

Edna's first job for Spellbound was right here at Thorton-Bryce Freight. Madame Maria Isadore, Spellbound Services' founder, led the incantation herself. The client had never hired witches before, and Madame Isadore's presence helped raise confidence. Her sister, Antonia Isadore, was also there. Edna was needed to stand on the third point in the triangle.

It was a seeking spell. If any of the newly arrived crates held damaged goods, the enchantment would mark them with deep green streaks.

Everything went as promised. Afterward, as they folded away their robes, Madame Isadore invited Edna to the post-meeting with Robert Bryce, the company's owner. Antonia had another engagement across town.

In the field, all Spellbound employees were required to wear business attire if they weren't in their robes, and the robes were only worn for spell casting. No jeans, sweats, or t-shirts. Madame Isadore set the example that day in her deep blue Eileen Fisher suit.

Edna received an advance on her first paycheck from Spellbound with instructions to buy nicer clothes. "I want you to carry yourself better," said Madame Isadore. "They expect to see us with terrible hair and ratty black cloaks, hunched around a cauldron. Or standing in front of a gingerbread house wearing old apron dresses. We must shatter this idea. That starts with a smart, tailored jacket." Madame Isadore carried just enough of a Castilian accent to put seasoning on the words, to make them special.

Robert Bryce was edgy at that meeting, something Edna would see often in new clients. "Sorry, Madame Isadore. I'm talking too much."

"Please, call me 'Maria.'"

"Maria, then. Your work is remarkable. They've checked fourteen of the marked crates so far and, sure enough, each has at least one problem item inside. This will save us a lot of trouble."

"But, Mr. Bryce, this is why you brought us here, yes?"

"Call me Bob, please. I hope you won't be insulted, but for this first job, my crew will check everything. Full inventory, just so I really know it worked. This is still very new to me."

"This is very new to you, Bob," said Madame Isadore, "but it is very, very old to the world."

"Yes, yes it is. I bet you run into a lot of misconceptions out there, right? People probably think you've got broomsticks and talking cats. Black magic stuff."

"Oh, excuse me," said Edna, "but no one says 'black magic' anymore. We call it 'ink.'" Madame Isadore's gaze snapped to Edna. "Sorry, I shouldn't interrupt."

"Please to forgive our young Miss Perry," said Madame Isadore. "She is very new to the world." Madame Isadore pulled some papers out of her bag. "Now, let's talk about the new ways Spellbound Services can help Thorton-Bryce Freight."

✦✦✦✦✦✦

On Edna's return, Daniel Santiago confirmed that the gauntcast found the site clear of ink. No bad juju from competing covens, no bad charms among the personnel. The circle and glyphs were drawn properly on the floor and each witch and warlock stood ready in their robes. "Excellent," said Edna, taking her place in the scissor lift. "Let's have a last look and get started."

She raised the lift and studied the loading bay, shifting her robes so they didn't get tangled in the works. From here, she could see into all three of the empty intermodal containers. Each had 2,400 cubic feet of capacity.

Laid out neatly on the bay's floor was enough cargo to fill five such containers, and it was the coven's job to fit it all into three. This would require a well-executed tessellation spell.

The fee for this magical service was $15,000, a bargain compared to the cost of shipping two extra containers all the way to China. The national covens didn't offer this service anymore. Larger freight companies paid them a fortune to teleport their goods. That was an intricate spell, requiring 39 casters at both the departure and the destination points.

There were limits. Teleportation only worked for non-organic freight, and printed material often became unreadable in the process. But the shippers who could afford it got the advantage of instant conveyance. Plus, clients loved the sparks and ozone smell when their wares popped into existence halfway across the world.

Spellbound Services was a local company. Madame Isadore employed less than a hundred witches and warlocks. Their emphasis was on craft and personal service, specializing in freight. The Isadore family had been managing freight as far back as the 1500s in Spain.

"With a smaller circle of clients comes a smaller circle of needs," Madame Isadore would say. "That makes more successes. It's not storybook magic, but there is a happy ending with success." It was traditional magic at traditional rates. And for a lot of companies, like Thorton-Bryce Freight, it was a perfect fit.

From the scissor lift, Edna gave a nod to Finch, the security chief. He made certain everyone in the gallery turned off their laptops and phones, then gave Edna an awkward thumbs-up.

She formed her fingers into a Shipton Knot, then moved her fists toward the coven. Every third witch sang low as the others swung their pendulums. As Edna watched and listened, she felt the oxycodone smoothing her ragged edges. She was careful to time her dose with the start of the gauntcast. If it was still dissolving, the tablet wouldn't show.

Her gaze shifted to the cargo. Most of the pallets held home electronics. There were also stacks of flat-pack furniture and over a thousand crates of bicycle parts. As her casters sang the tones, she spoke her right words and shaped the song around the goods. All twelve were singing now, modulating higher as the pendulums kept time.

Edna's eyes went silver as the spell gave her truer vision. She saw the auditory material surrounding the cargo. Her voice gave shape to the song, weaving it through all the containers. The voices became one, thirteen witches pulling a single note.

Then, a piece at a time, all the pallets and parts gathered in the air. They moved up and back, trading places and flipping end-over-end until each found its place in the song.

The floating cargo formed a geometric pattern, a three-dimensional mosaic. Edna moved her hands, and the whole lot glided into the containers, pulled along by the auditory thread. Without a scratch or dent, everything fit perfectly. The tessellation was successful.

One at a time, the voices dropped out, leaving only Daniel Santiago's as he sang the doors shut and sealed them. A Spellbound Services agent in Qingdao would use a jade whistle to open the doors and unpack the goods after the shipment arrived.

There were no sparks or ozone, but everyone in the gallery burst into applause at the spell's completion.

✦✦✦✦✦✦

Robert Bryce walked Edna to her car, carrying the container of pendulums as she rolled her suitcase. "So, you're back in two weeks?"

Edna used her free hand to check the calendar on her phone. "Yes, it's here. No fee, that one is part of the service contract."

Bryce smiled. "I like that." Her car door popped open, and Edna started piling things into the passenger seat. As she took the pendulums from Bryce, her phone chirped with a text from Madame Isadore.

"It's the boss," Edna said, looking at the message. "I've got to get to the office."

"You guys use text messages?"

"It's more dependable than telepathy. Plus, there's a paper trail. See you in a few weeks, Bob."

✦✦✦✦✦✦

Spellbound Services had a small space in a professional building, a few desks and a few doors. The tapestry covering the back wall of the meeting room was the only clue that this place was different from the real estate office down the hall.

Edna walked in and stored the pendulums in the supply cabinet. Antonia was the only person in view, scribbling as a client droned over her headset. She smiled at Edna then motioned toward the meeting room. Edna pointed to herself and the door; Antonia gave her a silent go-ahead. Hearing voices inside, Edna entered slowly.

Madame Isadore, alone in the room, motioned for Edna to take a seat as she finished up with the vendor on the speakerphone.

"So, that's four sets total?" asked the disembodied voice.

"Yes, Martin," said Madame Isadore. The main table was mostly bare, except for a few boxes and a set of crystals laid out on a piece of lavender flannel. "Four sets of twelve quartz, and each set needs a hardback case. I can have them next week?"

"Yes. By the way, did you get a chance to look at—"

"Sorry Martin, my next meeting has arrived." Madame Isadore rolled her eyes and flapped one hand like a bird beak. "Email me the invoice and you can tell me about this other thing in the cover letter, yes?"

"Um, yes. Thanks again. Goodbye, Maria, always nice to talk with you."

"And you, Martin. Goodbye." The speaker phone went quiet. Madame Isadore's hand hovered over the device.

"Do I need to hang up?" she asked. "Edna, can you make sure this is off?" Edna pulled the speakerphone over and saw they were disconnected. Madame Isadore put the sample crystals back in their cases.

"It's off," said Edna. The lift from the oxycodone was fading. She thought about taking another, but for now she would stick to her plan. That meant waiting until tonight.

"Good," said Madame Isadore. "That man has the best prices, the best things, but he won't stop talking." She set the cases aside and found Edna staring at the tapestry behind her chair.

It was easy to get lost inside the flowers and meandering patterns embroidered into the wall-sized affair. Madame Isadore's voice pulled her out of it. "So, Edna, today went well?"

"Yes," said Edna, finding her way back into the room. "Daniel Santiago, he's really stepping up."

"Good. I am becoming less wary of these warlocks. Slowly, though. I've seen too many men use the darker magics. Perhaps my view is ancient, yes? Maybe this is no longer true."

"The gauntcasts will catch any ink if it's there," said Edna.

"This word, 'ink,' rather than 'black magic,'" said Madame Isadore, "it has grown on me. 'Black magic' makes people think of the Devil. Stone altars, blood, demons. In truth, it is more subtle."

"Intent," said Edna. "Any spell is dark if it's cast with dark intent. Making a person love you, punishing someone."

"Or even lies." Madame Isadore's tone had changed. "Lies are dark. Yes, I like this word, 'ink.' Ink makes stains and ugly spots. Quite often, permanent. 'Ink' is a good word."

Christ, Edna thought, *does she know? She knows. Why else would she say that?* She tried to spend four times as long exhaling as she spent inhaling.

Madame Isadore pulled a cedar box to the center of the table. The lid was carved with a herringbone pattern, and a simple bronze hasp held it closed.

"My lace," said Madame Isadore. The hasp clicked and the lid raised up. The box was full of whole pieces and fragments, mostly white or black, but there were reds and yellows as well. Madame Isadore removed each of them from the box with great care, her thin hands spreading them out on the table. "Old. Older than me if you can imagine such a thing. So intricate, so lovely. Real Spanish lace."

She drew a white mantilla across her hands. "Did you know that most of what they call 'Spanish lace' was not made in Spain? Any lace that moved through a Spanish port, like Barcelona or Castellon, was called 'Spanish,' no matter where it was made. Then they could charge five times more for it, no matter how clumsy or cheap."

Edna paid close attention, doing her best to breathe, to calm her mind. She felt caught. Madame Isadore unrolled a wide, rose-patterned ribbon. "So, for many years, nearly all of the lace in the world came to Spain first, then to its actual destination."

She returned the ribbon to the table, then held up a white scrap with gold highlights. One of her fingers traced the lines. "Of course, real Spanish lace, the pieces we created locally, those were superior. The rest of it was a lie." Her gaze shifted to Edna. "Hold out your hand."

Edna reached out an unsteady hand and the white scrap with gold highlights was laid across her palm. It felt like an enormous responsibility. Madame Isadore calmed her. "It's not as fragile as I make it out to be, dear. Do you like it?"

The precision, the winding and tensions keeping the strands in place, Edna could sense an energy coming off the scrap. "Yes," she said. "It's lovely. I can feel it, the work. It must have taken months."

Antonia corrected her. "It took more than a year, Edna Perry." Edna had no idea she had come into the room. "My thinnest needles. Spool after spool of thread so fine that no one knows how to make it anymore. It felt like I was tugging them forever."

"This is all that's left of a lovely shawl Antonia made for a wealthy, terrible woman," said Madame Isadore. "When this lady got tired of wearing it, she cut it up to make doilies, the fool."

Antonia's eyes narrowed. "She brought the pieces back to me, upset because they were unraveling. She tore the shawl apart and then she wanted her money back."

"That's awful," said Edna.

The Isadore sisters shared a smile. "We returned every last coin, a total refund," said Madame Isadore, "but the money was disgraced. Bad luck came with it."

"The disgrace spread, infecting her fortunes," said Antonia. "Everything she bought turned against her. Expensive meals made her sick. Dresses and makeup made her ugly. Soon, we didn't see her anymore. It was as if she faded away. We managed to stitch the lace into smaller pieces, cuffs and collars mostly. It didn't go to waste."

"This bit was too small to make anything," said Madame Isadore, "but it was pretty, so it went in my box."

The lace held Edna's attention as she rotated the scrap in her hand. She was drawn to the pattern, like she was with the tapestry. For a time, no one made a sound.

Then Edna broke the silence. "You know," she said. "You know all of it and that's why I'm here. That's why both of you are here." It felt like someone else was speaking, giving away her most secret thoughts.

"Yes," said Antonia, "my sister and I know that something pulls on you, always. A harsh tether. We have been waiting, Edna Perry. Waiting for you to make it better."

They knew. Everything. A big wave was rising, and Edna couldn't dive under it.

"When we worked as healers, we saw this in the field army hospitals," said Madame Isadore. "Later, in the cities, New Orleans, San Francisco, it was the same. And here we are again."

"It is the pull of opium, the poppy's liquor," said Antonia. "You are not using a pipe or a syringe. You are using tablets in a dainty case, but it is the same. And as you take these pills, you still feel the tugging. You think, 'How long will it last?' or 'When can I get more?'"

"My sister is speaking to you, Edna Perry. Please look at her," said Madame Isadore. Edna raised her eyes from the lace to its creator.

"The opium, it is the last thing you think of before you sleep. The first thing you think of when you wake." Antonia paused, seeing something new. "No, even before you wake. Your sleep is filled with calamities. You can no longer dream."

Madame Isadore pushed a box of tissues to Edna. "Stop crying, dear. You are in our employ, an asset. We do not want to lose you."

"I don't want to be lost. But this is everything I've been afraid of. And it's happening. It's happening right now." Edna held the lace tight in one hand as she pulled a tissue with the other.

"Face it then," said Antonia. "You must be the proud, strong witch. Refuse the poppy's call and see things as they are."

"I'm so sorry," said Edna.

"Take that pill case out of your bag," said Madame Isadore.

"Yes," said Edna, standing, "yes, I'm going to go and flush them right now."

"Please," said Antonia, "sit down." As Edna dropped back into her seat, Madame Isadore eased the piece of lavender flannel across the table.

"Put the pill case on this," she said. Edna obeyed. "Are these the last of the tablets? All that you have?"

"Yes," said Edna, "but I can get more. On Monday."

Antonia's eyes went momentarily grey. "You will not," she said. Edna knew that the pharmacy had lost her prescription.

Madame Isadore started shaping the flannel around the tortoise-shell pill case. Antonia handed her sister a needle and thread. Edna wondered where they came from.

Madame Isadore's fingers dipped the needle round and round. Each move was startling, quick, and perfect. "My sister's work is outstanding," said Antonia. "That scrap, give it to me." Edna handed the white lace to Antonia who, in turn, passed it to her sister.

The needle flipped and darted, making the lace part of the work. Edna got lost in the flashes of the steel and fabric. She heard Antonia speak.

"When I was young," she said, "I was never without my small vial of Laudanum. It was meant to ease the pain of the soldiers in my care, but with the war all around, the men in charge of the field hospital didn't notice when a few ounces went missing.

"After the war, like many of the soldiers, I kept taking the Laudanum." Antonia had moved behind her sister, watching her work, adrift in the same needle dance that captivated Edna Perry. "Maria stayed away from it. After a time, she stayed away from me. Eventually, everyone stayed away and there was only me and my little vial. It was like that for years. I asked Maria why we didn't see each other. She said she couldn't watch me die."

"Antonia quit two years later, and she cheated for one year more," said Madame Isadore. "We started speaking again four years after that." She snapped the thread with her teeth and looked at the object's edges with critical eyes. "This is good, yes?"

She handed it to Antonia. "Yes, Maria," she said, scrutinizing. "It is lovely." With that, Antonia handed what looked like a square sachet to Edna.

The pill case made a muffled rattle as she took it. The flannel had been sewn around the case with a seam so tight it was invisible. The white and gold lace was inlayed over the lavender background. "It's beautiful," said Edna. "Is this a mojo bag?"

The Isadore sisters laughed. "Are you at a carnival?" asked Antonia. "Those are for palm readers. They sell them to fools."

"It just keeps your pills," said Madame Isadore. "That flannel is triple woven, one of the thread runs is waxed. Tough, waterproof, should last forever."

"Especially with Maria's stitching," said Antonia. "You would need something sharp to get it open. But you don't want to ruin my lace, do you?"

"No," said Edna, remembering the fate of the last woman who ruined this lace. "It's a treasure."

"And don't put it through the wash," said Madame Isadore. "Listen dear, this is over now. And you are still alive. Still employed. Do not flush these pills."

"No. You must keep them with you, always," said Antonia.

"I can't get rid of them?" asked Edna.

"You can never really be rid of them," said Antonia. "But you can keep choosing not to take them."

"Yes. You will have them, like a tattoo, for the rest of your life," said Madame Isadore. "Refuse their call, see through their lies, and this is how you find power. Peace will come in time, perhaps a long time. But until then, you have us."

"You have already stopped taking the opium," said Antonia. "You stopped hours ago. Starting again, that will be hard. You'll need scissors, maybe a knife. Or you'll need to charm some idiot doctor. Then you'll need to hide the ink as the stains grow. To me, these things sound harder than quitting. Quitting is not doing anything at all."

Edna noticed the pendant on Antonia Isadore's necklace. It was a large, glass teardrop with a platinum bale. There was a bubble moving near the top, as the glass held a tiny bit of liquid inside.

Madame Isadore took Edna's hand. "So, my strong proud witch, would you like to stay with us tonight?"

Edna had stayed at their big house in the hills twice before, when they had large projects coming that needed materials prepared. It was nice, lots of rooms and history.

"Yes," said Edna. "Yes, I think I should, thank you."

✦✦✦✦✦✦

That night, Edna dreamt of her childhood. On a school trip to the Botanical Gardens, she saw lizards sunning in the walkways. When her class came nearer, the lizards darted away to the safety of the flowerbeds. As she passed by, each one called her name.

She would sleep six hours in a row, and tomorrow she would wake up hungry for the first time in years. She would tie a string around her neck to let her not-a-mojo-bag hang hidden under her clothes.

Edna Perry was a strong, proud witch. She was scared as hell.

But she had a chance. Because she wasn't "without."

SavagePlanets
Where Dreams & Nightmares Collide

LEARN MORE

READ, SUBMIT, IMAGINE BEYOND YOUR LIMITS...
RETRIEVE COLORS NO LONGER SEEN, STOLEN BY SAGITTARIUS A*

THE JEWEL OF THE WAVES, THE DIADEM OF THE SKY
BY JARED OLIVER ADAMS

The missing person report chimes while I am carefully selecting a grapefruit from a vendor along the Bridgeway. A chill climbs my neck under my sweaty hijab, but I double-blink to scan the report summary anyway.

As the words of the summary superimpose themselves over my field of vision, the flooded city of Chennai fuzzes behind them. The brightly-colored solar tapestries swaying from the surrounding high-rises blur to grey, and the vibrant coral landscape that covers the ground like a carpet goes monochrome as well. Even the glare off the water becomes less intense.

Priya Yadav. Twenty-two. Neuralink went offline eleven days ago, but she was just reported missing this morning. Works as a mechanic for the city, servicing Chennai's sanitation robots.

"Madame Gitali?" asks the vendor. "Are you quite well?"

I've frozen in place with the grapefruit lifted in front of me.

"I...yes, Mablevi, " I lie. "I will take these. Thank you."

When people boil their neuralinks, they are usually in deep trouble within 24 hours. With children, you are notified almost immediately when a link goes offline. But, since Priya Yadav is an adult, I don't get called until someone submits a report. Eleven days!

I pay Mablevi with a two-finger flick in his direction, then tuck the groceries into my bag, but my eyes keep sliding to the sparkling water below, once more at full shine since I exited reading mode.

Chennai, The Jewel of the Waves, they say.

Mixed with the normal bustle of pedestrians and shoppers, painters along the Bridgeway endeavor to capture the beauty of the reefs below, while small groups of city planners from across the ocean gawk at technical overlays of the same view, showing the hidden wave turbines, perhaps, or the server cooling systems or who-knows-what-else.

My overlay is far more grim, and there's no software involved. Snorkeling down, staking yourself within the coral, and popping a neurotoxin has become the most popular suicide method in Chennai. It's so popular, in fact, people travel from across India just to kill themselves here. Suicide tourism.

Hair, it billows in the water just like the plants in the reef. And fish, well, they are not picky about food.

The images of dozens of bodies found this way wash through my mind like the tide. Memories aren't like nueralink data; you can't just swipe them from your field of vision, can't blur them.

I say a prayer to Allah, then apply for the autowarrants I need. The simple task centers me. A couple minutes and I have an address.

I find the first stairs that lead to the Underbridge rail and force myself not to look down at the glittering coral vista through the glass walls as I descend.

I try to believe there is still time for Priya Yadav, but my mind whispers: *eleven days.*

~~~~ ▲ ~~~~

I always keep a spare uniform rolled in my bag when I go out. It's a simple outfit: a khaki shirt with the red flame of the Department of Investigations stitched onto the pocket, and matching pants with a red stripe down the leg. Not exactly military-crisp after being in my bag, and I don't have the proper boots with me, just my sandals, which is mildly embarrassing.

But to get boots, I'd need to go back to my flat, and who knows if the half-hour spent doing that will be the crucial half-hour I needed to bring Priya Yadav home safely?

I cannot risk it.

The sound of a shakuhachi flute lilts through the air of the rail platform as I tensely wait for the train. It is a soothing counterpoint to the full missing person report, which is reading itself to me at triple speed. He's blind, the flute player, and quite elderly. Japanese, I believe. His body ebbs and flows gently with the music as he presides over the large bronze pan that proclaims him a Busker Monk. I've always found something pure about their Order. To subsist entirely off gifts of passersby, no government sponsorship, no basic income, has an antiquated courage to it.

I offload my produce to him, and he nods his thanks as he continues to play.

According to the report, the month before Priya's link went dead, she filed a request to use all of her accumulated vacation and conservation days, forty-two in all. This was a pattern she followed every six months or so. She'd chosen mountain conservation as her volunteer assignment, which meant just to discharge her duties, she had to spend precious vacation hours to travel to a mountain range.

Me, I do local waterway conservation for my con hours, which is mostly plucking litter from the side of a boat. Also, to be honest, I usually pay a teenager from my mosque to do it, because who has the time?

Priya Yadav, apparently.

She belonged to a tight-knit group of mountain enthusiasts. They'd had an expedition set to start yesterday, tracking eagle populations in the Vindhya range. They'd been the ones to report her missing. The Office of Investigations AI interviewed them, and the sheer volume of manic details in the report suggests none of them were involved in her disappearance.

The AI has flagged a certain bit, though, and I get to it just as I'm stepping across the gangplank into the Skimmer-Train. "Possible suicide note," says the AI in its clinical voice. My stomach collapses at the words and I stumble into my seat before I switch to visual mode so I can read it myself.

I cannot take the AI reading me another suicide note.

Hey Mountebanks,

 I guess by now you have figured out I'm not coming. Zaman is probably freaking about having one less pack drone, and Dhanashree is quietly grumbling about how she's got to shift meals around to cover the food I was supposed to bring. Sorry, guys.

 There's something I have to do, something I have been planning a long time. That's all I can say about it. Whatever happens, promise me you won't blame yourselves, okay? Especially you, Hetika. You crazies are the best friends a person could have. If I don't come back, it doesn't have anything to do with you. Got it?

 If you miss my snoring too much, I bet Jaheel still has that recording she took to embarrass me. You can always play it on loop to help you sleep.

 Love to you, my dear friends.   -Priya

I reread the note twice before my heart stops pounding. The nostalgia of a suicide note is there. The pleas for friends not to blame themselves too. But it is less . . . declarative.

If I don't come back, it doesn't have anything to do with you. Got it?

She says "if."

Not a variation on the horrifyingly cliché "I've gone to become one with the reef." No, she says "if."

I take a breath to steady myself. There is still hope. And I've been so absorbed in the note that my stop is already coming up.

It's time to see her apartment.

~~~~ ▲ ~~~~

The Slumstacks lie at the far edge of my jurisdiction. Actually, they lie at the far edge of everybody's jurisdiction. The districts overlap here like a Venn Diagram, both to share the greater caseload and to let the captains blame one another when things go wrong.

The Bridgeway connects to it, yes, but the Underbridge rail hasn't worked here for a decade, and all the foot traffic has to squeeze between the shacks slumped against the bridge walls.

Below the Bridgeway, the reef has not taken here. Too much pollution, even with people and robots working nonstop to filter it out. The Development Authority eventually gave up and installed a water barrier to keep the algae blooms from spreading to healthier areas.

The stacks themselves were designed with staggered balconies to allow for mango, banana, and lemon trees, but

Jared Oliver Adams

few of those trees still exist. Instead, the residents have enclosed the balconies with pulpboard for more space.

At the clogged doorway to Priya's building, the Helpnet Sergeant waits, arms crossed over his orange kurta. He presses his lips together under his matching orange-dyed moustache.

Helpnetters love to be conspicuous.

"Antagonist," he says with a tiny nod of his balding head.

"Antagonist," I echo back with an equally reserved nod. Together, the Helpnet and the Department of Investigations represent a unified whole, one seeking mercy, one seeking penalty. He's got the same flame sigil on the breast of his kurta that I do, though his is white. It has something to do with the two-faced Hindu god of fire, but that's about all I care to know. May Allah bring all pagans to repentance.

For missing persons, the Helpnetters and the DI work together, but there's always this theatric production of appearing as adversaries. It helps the credibility of the Helpnet, supposedly.

Plus, some of them are jerks.

"If your sandals will hold together, perhaps you will follow me?" says the Sergeant blandly.

I pinch a smile at him and repress the desire to make fun of his moustache. "As you will," I say.

Each of the towers here has a hospital at the Bridgeway level, but they, like everything here, are overcrowded. The sergeant leads a weaving path through the gurneys and medcarts in the lobby. An elderly white woman is dozing as she receives dialysis beside the door to the lift. She doesn't wake when the lift chimes for us, but she's breathing. Yes, breathing.

I pack into the lift with the sergeant and a half-dozen others. "You have come on an auspicious day," he says. "One of the lifts is operational." This brings a chorus of laughter.

Everybody is always joking with the Helpnetters. That, of course, is their function, to preempt crime with their joviality, to be the friend you call when things go wrong. It's hard not to resent that though. People tend to grow very guarded when they see my DI khakis.

Sometimes I feel like the water barrier, sifting out the sludge of suicides and abductions so the Helpnetters can laugh on the lift with their friends.

Everybody has a function.

The lift disgorges us into a crowded hallway. Every sort of household activity is on display. We step over the outstretched legs of kids sitting against the wall, doing schoolwork. Then we squeeze past a quartet of old men crouching around an ornate Pachisi board painted in the direct center of the concrete floor. Next, a Filipino woman tends a Tandoori oven shoulder-to-shoulder with a white man searing vegetables on a stovetop.

The ventilation ducts that snake into the nearby door are not up to any fire or safety code on the planet. The sergeant notices me noticing and silently dares me to say something.

I don't take the dare.

But I do ask the question that has to be asked. "What is Priya Yadav doing living here? She's got a job that pays far above basic dole."

"Subleasing," says the sergeant. "You know how it goes."

It's a standard feature of the Slumstacks. A family fortunate enough to get an official housing assignment doubles up with another family so they can rent out the space unofficially, splitting the money between them.

"But why do you allow it?" I ask.

His eyes flash. "I *allow it* because when the ancient food pulp machines jam every other week, she spends hours elbows-deep in other peoples' rotting food to make them synthesize again. In other words, *she* is a helpful member of our community."

His tone implies pretty heavily that I am not.

I hold up my hands in defense. If I continue to dig into why she lives here, this conversation will get heated quickly. Why wouldn't someone want to live here? What are you implying?

"Can you tell me anything else about her?" I ask.

"She runs the stairs every morning with a very large backpack and some sort of breathing apparatus. I had to assign her an individual time, because the other stair walkers kept getting knocked by her pack when she passed."

"Was she training for something?"

He bobbles his head. "She would not confide in me. Here is her door."

"Are you coming in as well?"

He smiles sharply. "I, of course, scanned the apartment down to the fiber before you came, but I have more pressing matters than watching over your shoulder."

I bite back a retort. This is the system. We're both paid by Chennai. He is doing his job. Rudely, yes. But rudeness should not beget rudeness. Allah loves those who control their rage.

"You serve this place well," I say, pressing hands together and bowing. "Thank you for serving me also."

"Bring her back safely," he says, like an older brother to his sister's suitor.

"In sha Allah," I murmur as he continues down the busy hallway.

God willing.

As I walk into the small concrete cube that is Priya's flat, I'm greeted by the smell of machine oil and an invite to uplink to her virtual overlay.

I click it, but task the overlay to my right eye only. This way, I can close my left eye to see her virtual space, and switch eyes to view her physical space. I've told some of my colleagues about this trick, and they think it's crazy, but it's the best way to compare the two.

The cosmetic changes a person makes to their virtual space says a lot about them. With Priya, my immediate sense is one of sparse frugality. In the physical world, she has no rugs over the concrete floor, only a tarp in the corner stacked with machine parts. The Department AI flags this as possible city property; apparently her boss mentioned some items brought home that needed to be returned.

Continuing the frugal theme, her virtual space is a stock overlay. *Italian Villa*, the third option on every basic menu.

Half the dorm rooms at University had this overlay. I've seen the same view of the Mediterranean with the same seagulls hundreds of times.

So where did all of Priya's money go? Some people rent a cheap place like this so they can splurge on overlay, but that obviously isn't the case. Was she simply a saver?

Did she just not care?

Here's an interesting thing: instead of a bed, she has a transparent tent. There is not even a mattress in the tent, just a pillow and a sleeping bag spread out over the hard concrete. It looks equally out of place in the Italian Villa as it does in her flat.

Who sleeps in a tent inside their apartment?

And if she boiled her link to live out some kind of back-to-nature fantasy, wouldn't she bring this stuff with her?

Let's see what other outdoor gear she has.

The closet door is a gilded mirror in the virtual world, but dull white pulpboard in the real one. It slides on a track to reveal a single clothes rack and many cubbies. A few coveralls that have seen a lot of use hang beside a lovely emerald green sari that has seen very little. Three hangers are bare though, and there is a lot of empty space left on that bar. Big enough for a giant backpack, maybe? No backpack in sight.

The cubbies suggest she at least had time to pack. There are entire cubbies empty, and judging by how crammed some of the others are, this is not their normal state.

But, then, there is a second tent here in a bag, so unless she has a third, she's not planning on camping.

The bathroom also reveals very little. She has a weather map on the wall where you can watch it from the toilet. It's centered on northern India, but I spot the Vindhya range there, which is where she was supposed to meet up with her friends.

She has no medications in the physical world that have been edited from the virtual one.

In fact, I see nothing that isn't mirrored exactly between the virtual and physical, and that's a problem, because it's usually the discrepancies that tell you the most.

I wander back to the kitchen area. A piece of pulpboard rests on the table, and it's got grooves etched into it, like she's been tracing the same pattern over and over again with her stylus. I scan it, but nothing pings. The concentric blobs tug at my memory, but I can't dredge up where I've seen them before.

I lean against the table and cast around the room, switching eyes: *Italian Villa*, concrete apartment, *Italian Villa*, concrete apartment. The real space has no windows. Used to let out into a balcony, but it's been walled off. Is that where the family lives who's subleasing to her? How do they get in and out? Through the adjacent apartment?

I make to leave, go track down the neighbor, but my foot kicks something under the table, something that does not show up in the Italian Villa.

I freeze, then bend down.

A mini-fridge?

No. About that size, but this is some kind of . . . air purifier, maybe? It's got a wide hose attached to the side.

"Alti-MAX," reads the logo.

I blink a picture over to my nueralink, and don't have to scroll far for this whole flat to make a lot more sense. This device simulates the low oxygen of high altitudes, and the hose connects to a variety of permanent or inflatable chambers.

Chambers like the transparent tent in which Priya's sleeping bag lies.

Allah favors the curious!

And look! "Alti-MAX" also makes a portable model for training that has a facemask.

That's what she's been doing on the stairs! She's training for high altitude.

I look again at the trace-marks on the pulpboard. Before you could 3-D model terrain, and before you could ask your nueralink what you were looking at anywhere on the planet, there were elevation maps. My uncle had one on his wall as an art piece.

Priya has traced this one over and over, committing it to memory in preparation for boiling her link.

The computer renders it in a matter of seconds once I give it the proper parameters: Mount Everest.

My jaw drops as the legal info on Everest arranges itself across my field of vision.

You try to trespass on Everest, and you're thrice doomed: once by Nepal, who governs the land it's on, once by the Sherpa people who care for the mountain itself and consider it holy, and once by the International Gaia Tribunal, which provides legal defense for natural heritage sites that have personhood equivalency.

Trespassing on Everest will earn you an internal nueralink embedded in your neck. No boiling that. There are fines too, and likely time working the fields at the rehabilitation farms. Might even be some isolation service like microplastic recovery in the open ocean. She'd definitely never get a city job again, much less be involved in any of her beloved mountain conservation expeditions.

She'd practically have to kill somebody to get a more severe punishment.

My gaze lowers to the flame on my shirt pocket.

It's not the white flame of mercy; I'm not in the Helpnet. By all protocol, I should send this up the chain so they can offload it to the proper Sherpa/Nepalese/Gaia authorities. Afterwards, I should leave with a clear conscience, having done my job.

But I can't.

Because I need to know first. I need to know why on Earth would she risk this.

So, I flip the place. I remove every drawer, collect hair samples in the bathroom, catalogue the machine parts on the tarp, check the air vents, x-ray her composter and the planters on her produce wall for things hidden in the soil, gather samples from the three core spots inside her food pulper.

I even go inside her clear tent, though there doesn't seem to be anything there. I've stopped switching back and forth between virtual and physical views until I'm leaving the tent and see a discolored spot on the inside tent-wall, a little glob of adhesive.

I switch to virtual view then to see a small photograph, only visible from inside the tent. It's old; the color is faded and the middle-aged African man smiling toothily at the camera is wearing old-fashioned winter clothes. The snowy slope in the background is Everest again, according to my nueralink.

On the ceiling of the tent is something else only visible from the inside: the words "because it is there . . .", another Everest reference, specifically climbing Everest to the summit. It's an emboldening sentiment, for sure, but not the sort of thing that would move somebody to this level of crime.

No, the picture is the more important find here, because the adhesive on the tent wall is real, which means this picture was so important that she took it with her.

I'm about to submit the picture to a database when a call comes in from City Sanitation.

"These aren't what we're looking for," says an annoyed woman without preamble, displaying the pictures I sent of the machine parts.

"That's all there is in the apartment."

"Then she stole very valuable equipment," she says. "She signed out an entire reef bot for home repair."

Unasked-for comes the vision of a teenage boy who committed suicide in the reef, a quadrupedal bot picking its spindly legs through the surrounding plant-life behind his waving corpse.

"There's nothing that big here," I say.

The woman hisses with annoyance and leaves the call before I can tell her to file an update to the report, an update that would add a grand larceny tag.

I look back at the picture of the African man.

Who are you, and what did you make Priya do?

～～～▲～～～

The refugee archive identifies the man as Samuel Greene. Escaped persecution in the former United States in the mid-21st century, before the country fractured.

Samuel Greene left for fear of his life along with nearly a million others. India took about 300,000 and employed them in an early iteration of the conservation corps. Greene went to Sikkim in Northern India. His job: cleaning up trash left by recreational mountain climbers.

Eventually, he got transferred to Nepal and worked on Everest, where he died a few years later. That's where the refugee database left it, but an archived news article told the rest of the story. A climbing disaster in the Khumbu Icefall killed Greene and three others in his conservation crew.

But not before he married a Nepalese woman.

The trail to Priya unfurls like one of those hidden-text novels they make you study in Higher Secondary school, the double-spaced ones with the invisible words in between the lines. The Nepalese woman, Ang Dawa Sherpa, crossed into India soon after the disaster and remarried. That was the visible text. But with the help of a few pictures and some simple date calculation, it was clear that she had either left Nepal pregnant or with an infant in her arms, Greene's baby.

Priya's grandmother.

Had she left Nepal in disgrace for marrying an American refugee? Or was she simply trying to escape her grief?

Either way, Priya is 1/8th Sherpa.

I call my commander and ask if he has any contacts with the Sherpa people.

～～～▲～～～

The ancient man I am eventually passed off to is named Wangchu Pasang Sherpa. He's got twinkling eyes that nest in a bed of wrinkles like dark birds' eggs, and a colorful knit hat. "Priya Yadav did apply to join the tribe, yes, but unfortunately her lineage was insufficient."

That strikes me as an injustice, but I don't mention it. "Did she ask for any other concession?"

"She asked for travel rights upon the face of Chomolungma."

He sees the confusion on my face.

"That is the true name of Everest," he explains.

Ah. "And she was denied?"

"Of course. Even the scientific operations granted travel rights are completed mostly by drone. She wished to walk on Chomolungma with her own feet. Alone. Which is dangerous as well as illegal."

"Dangerous?" I ask.

Wangchu Pasang Sherpa brays laughter unselfconsciously. "People died on the mountain when it was strewn with ropes and ladders and staffed with cooks. Now? Without that and with the icefall increasingly unstable? It is suicide."

The word hits me hard. Is that all this is? Suicide? Is the mountain her reef? Will she stake herself there?

I thank him hollowly and end the call.

I'm sitting cross-legged on the floor of her flat so I don't touch anything. Is this all that's left of Priya Yadav? This room that will subleased again the second her rent comes due?

The door opens.

"Ah, it seems you are finished with your snooping," says the Helpnet Sergeant with the orange mustache. "Or are you merely resting from the mental rigors of your *investigations*?"

I don't have the energy to continue this charade of rudeness. "Do you know anybody at Gaia?"

The sincerity strikes him silent. He rushes to come in and close the door.

"The Green Lawyers?"

"Yes."

"What could you possibly want with them?"

I don't stand. I don't want him to feel threatened. I stay in my spot and tell him everything, full disclosure.

When I'm done, he is stroking his ridiculous mustache with a faraway look.

"But you have not reported her?"

I give the vaguest wobble of my head.

"Why?"

"I don't know," I say.

He studies me. "I may have a contact with Gaia. What do you need them to do?"

I tell him. His eyebrows try to climb up his balding head. "Only if I get to watch," he says.

~~~~ ▲ ~~~~

The Gaia drone is a high-resolution camera set in a quadrotor that's modified to fly in the thin air above Everest. The Helpnet Sergeant has told his contact that he is using it to give a tour to Slumstack residents. "Which I will do when we are done with this, so I will not be a liar."

The drone is on a proscribed path; we aren't flying it. But we can toggle altitude to some degree and we have control of the camera.

Everest fills Priya's apartment, complete immersion mode. The clouds swirl around us, the wind whipping icy dust off the mountainside like spirits. The nueralink translates the wind to my skin, chapping my face and giving me the sensation that my hijab is flapping loose.

It takes over an hour to spot a blurry pair of shapes making their way up the mountain. Priya has sheathed her climbing clothes in Mirror Sheen so that she blends into the mountainside.

The reef-cleaning bot that spiders its way ahead of her isn't hidden as well. The solar fabric that's draped over its back is white, but it's not Mirror Sheen, and it trails a strange rope behind it, one with yellow tendrils that seem to anchor it to the ground. After Priya passes a section anchored thusly, she changes her clips to access the next section, and the tendrils suck back into the rope, leaving nothing but a quickly-fading outline in the ice.

"She is almost to where Camp III used to be," says Sergeant Chanesh, pointing to a data tag upslope.

We zoom as close to Priya as we can, close enough to see the joyful determination on her face under her sunglasses. Instead of the climbing pickaxe Green carried in his photo, she carries something that looks like some kind of industrial spatula.

I share a look across the gauzy sky with Chanesh before pulling up a search window. It's called a Gecko Stick. A marketing video shows a man using a pair of them to scale the glass side of a skyscraper.

"Look up the rope," says Chanesh.

The rope is harder to find, but when I do, I cringe. "It's pretty gross," I say to him, opening a window over the white face of the mountain to show an animation of how the rope uses the proteins in urine to create a sort of nano particle filament that spreads to anchor itself like the roots of a plant.

Chanesh snorts a laugh. "Efficient!" he says.

And, again, something that doesn't damage the mountain. They apparently used to drill bolts into the rock.

"Do you know what she does not have?" Chanesh asks.

"What?"

"Recording equipment. At least that I can spot. This is no show for others."

"Because it's there," I whisper.

He looks at me quizzically.

"I think she's planning on coming back," I say. "This whole thing, connecting to her past, challenging herself, it's between her and the mountain. I bet she comes back and never tells a soul."

He considers, floating in the Everest air. "Will you prosecute her for the missing robot when she returns?"

"It won't be missing when she returns, will it?"

He grins. "No. No, it won't."

"Then let's make sure she returns," I say.

Below us, Priya Yadav labors up the mountain of her ancestors, a culmination of training, sacrifice, and extreme risk, made more extreme by the fact that she doesn't have a neuralink to call for help.

But we do.

She doesn't think to look up at the drone. Her thermal hood probably mutes any sound the rotors make that isn't blown away by the wind.

She imagines herself alone.

She's not.

"I'll take the first shift," I say.

"I will bring some food when I return," he says, and leaves me to Priya and the glorious icy mountainside, which shines in the sun like a diadem.

Jared Oliver Adams

Flybys, Launch Windows, and Selfies with the Earth and Moon:

The Artemis I Flight from the Perspective of a Member of the Trajectory-Design Team

By Robert E. Harpold

Artemis I

Artemis I was the first full test flight of the new Orion spacecraft, which was designed to return people to the Moon. If certain aspects of this flight had failed, we would have had to repeat it before the spacecraft could be certified to carry people. Our main objective was to test the heat-shield at speeds it would experience from a lunar return, but we also wanted to test every system aboard the spacecraft and recover the vehicle. If you followed the news about the flight, you know it achieved every major objective and several objectives that weren't proposed until mid-flight.

Artemis I, and the Artemis program in general, was possible because of many teams consisting of many individuals who dedicated themselves to the mission. Each team focused on its own subsystem, and the individuals within those teams further focused on detailed aspects of that subsystem. It took thousands of people, spread across the country and in other countries, to make Artemis I a success.

I have little knowledge about other teams because I was siloed within my own specialty within my own team, but hopefully describing our work will give you an idea of the work and enthusiasm of every team who supported Artemis I. I also hope it gives you at least a hint of what it was like to be part of this project and a sense of pride at what humans can accomplish when we push ourselves to explore.

Trajectory Design

Our team designed the trajectories, the path the spacecraft would take from the Earth to the Moon and back again. In order to prove the Orion spacecraft could carry humans, the trajectory had to satisfy several mission objectives, including testing the heat shield at lunar-return velocities, demonstrating that Orion's propulsion, navigation, communications, and other systems could operate in the space environment, and returning the vehicle to a designated landing site.

Jacob Williams designed the original trajectory over a decade ago. Orion's destination was a Distant Retrograde Orbit (DRO) around the Moon, an interesting orbit where the spacecraft is actually in Earth orbit, but, from the perspective of an observer on the Moon, it would look like the spacecraft was orbiting the Moon backward.

In the nominal mission plan, five major burns would be performed (Figure 1). Ninety minutes after launch, the Interim Cryogenic Propulsion Stage (ICPS) would perform the Trans-Lunar Injection (TLI) burn to send Orion to the Moon. During the flyby of the Moon, Orion would perform the Outbound Powered Flyby (OPF) burn which, with the assistance of the Moon's gravity, would send Orion on a path toward the DRO. It would then perform the Distant Retrograde orbit Insertion (DRI) burn to enter the DRO. Six days later, it would perform the Distant Retrograde orbit Departure (DRD) burn to head back to the Moon, and then perform the Return Powered Flyby (RPF) burn to use the Moon's gravity to return to Earth.

Tim Dawn updated the original trajectory to account for additional mission constraints. One of those constraints was making certain Orion's landing occurred during daylight, which would help recovery operations. To achieve this objective, the mission duration could be between 26 – 28 days or 38 – 42 days. Max Widner wrote software that would select the mission duration that achieved all mission objectives and minimized fuel usage.

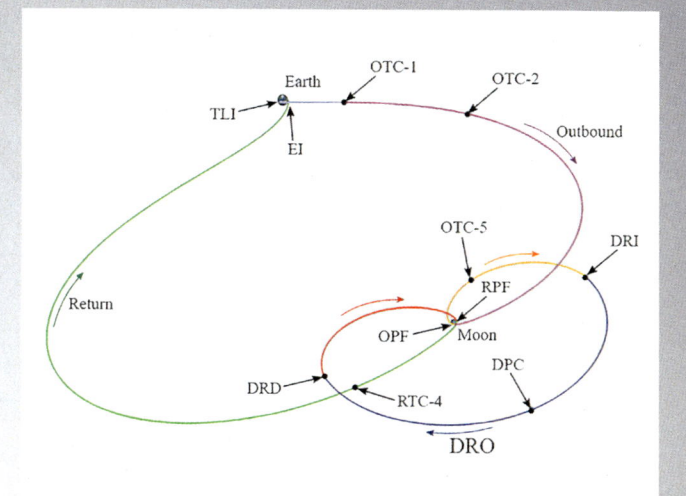

Figure 1. Artemis I Trajectory. TLI = TransLunar Injection, OTC = Outbound Trajectory Correction, OPF = Outbound Powered Flyby, DRO = Distant Retrograde Orbit, DRI = Distant Retrograde orbit Insertion, DRD = Distant Retrograde orbit Departure, RPF = Return Powered Flyby, RTC = Return Trajectory Correction, EI = Entry Interface. Figure courtesy of Batcha, Amelia L., et al. "Artemis I Trajectory Design and Optimization." 2020 AAS/AIAA Astrodynamics Specialist Conference. No. AAS 20-649. 2020.

But, since the Earth-Moon geometry changes, the trajectory would change due to the launch date, and differences in launch azimuth would cause changes throughout the two-hour launch window. Some trajectories would violate the constraint for length of time in eclipse (when either the Earth or Moon are blocking the sunlight on the spacecraft), which would deplete the battery-power reserves and thermally stress the spacecraft. If those eclipses weren't eliminated or reduced below the limit, Orion couldn't fly those trajectories, which would result in the loss of available launch dates. Sarah Smallwood developed an eclipse-mitigation algorithm to recover those launch dates by adding correction burns or inclining the DRO.

Before flight, we also needed to know the available contingency options. One set of possibilities was the spacecraft missing a major burn, delaying the burn, or the engine only performing part of the burn. Brian Killeen developed software to determine a correction burn that would return the spacecraft to the nominal trajectory in those situations.

We also needed to protect for the possibility of the Space Launch System (SLS) rocket or the ICPS engine not performing their burns for the full durations, which would result in Orion being placed on the wrong trajectory. Colin Brown and Tim developed several types of alternate missions, some flying by the Moon and others remaining in Earth orbit, that would still achieve some or all of the main mission objectives.

We also needed to be ready to bring the spacecraft home early in case of mission-ending spacecraft failures. I developed software to find abort trajectories for each phase of the mission for different types of failures. For each combination of launch date and time, we generated hundreds of abort trajectories. Within each month, we would typically have between 10 and 15 available days to launch, and we would generate abort trajectories for five epochs each day, so we generated thousands of abort trajectories for each month. This amount of data became unwieldy, so Colin wrote a database to store them and provide efficient access to them.

In addition, Jeff Gutkowski was our team lead, Randy Eckman wrote trajectory-design tools, Amelia Batcha was our main analyst studying the feasibility of each trajectory, Badejo Adebonojo ran the missed-burn cases, Elizabeth Williams wrote software to plot different data for each trajectory, Josh Geiser joined our team shortly before launch, and Matt Horstman and Jacob generated off-nominal trajectories in the office after launch. Most of us worked on future Artemis missions at the same time, but I am only listing the tasks we performed specifically for Artemis I.

Our team had fun with the tool names. There was Damocles, an ominous name that raised some eyebrows. That name inspired Elizabeth to call her plotting tool Plotacles. We also had a trajectory vending machine, RoboCopPy, and RATGATOR. Similarly, one of the teams in Mission Control named all their tools after Batman characters.

Every month until we launched, our team cranked out all the necessary trajectories (nominal and off-nominal) and presented them to management and our flight controller counterparts. This work was in addition to our development of new contingency options we kept realizing we needed, which continued up to the day we launched.

Because of our trajectory work, the flight controllers in Mission Control needed our team to be on console in the Mission Evaluation Room.

MER and TARGO

Most people have heard of Mission Control in Houston. It's the room where the Flight Director and the flight controllers, each in charge of their own specialty, help operate the spacecraft and troubleshoot any anomalies during flight. Each flight controller is supported by a counterpart in a back room (called the Multi-Purpose Support Room or MPSR, pronounced 'mip-ser') with whom they are in constant contact. Where a flight controller is in charge of integrating their system with the entire team, the people in the MPSR focus on work related to their specific subsystem.

There is also a back backroom called the MER (Mission Evaluation Room, pronounced 'mer') for the people who designed, built, and/or tested the subsystems. They monitor their systems and help the flight controllers troubleshoot anomalies. For an Apollo 13 analogy, there was a time where NASA engineers had to figure out how to fit the command module's square carbon-dioxide-filter canister into the round slot for the lunar module's canister. That problem is an extreme example of the kind of work the MER would be called upon to do. There were twenty consoles in the MER (Figure 2), and at any given time, there were about thirty people in the room.

Our team's console in the MER was called TARGO (Trajectory Analysis, RetarGeting, and Optimization). We primarily supported the Flight Dynamics Officer (FDO, pronounced like the dog name), the Mission Control console in charge of the spacecraft trajectory. The FDOs have been treated with high respect since the early days of human spaceflight, and, from my experience interacting with them, they deserve every bit of that respect. During flight, we provided them with updated nominal trajectories and off-nominal options for each phase of the mission, as well as performing additional analysis when requested.

For another Apollo 13 analogy, in the movie, there is a scene where Gene Kranz points to a chalkboard and draws the two options available to them: turn around right away or loop around the Moon and take longer to return. If that flight happened today, TARGOs would have been the ones to have told the team about those options before the flight.

Brian and Randy led our training. They assigned each of us to prepare lessons on our specialties and even gave us a written test, just like in our school days (it was an open-book, take-home test). The fun part of training, though, was the simulations.

In the simulations, our testers would create scenarios with different systems failing so we could train to fix the problems or find a way to perform the mission despite the problems. The simulations gave us valuable experience in interacting with our flight controller counterparts and other MER teammates and learning things like speaking on the appropriate loops and not talking when the Flight Director is talking. We even had three simulations that lasted 36 hours each which let us practice passing files between shifts and having team members pick up a problem from where one shift left off and then transferring that work to the next shift. It reminded me of what I'd read about training during the Apollo era.

Figure 2. Ops Suite 3, the room where the MER team did its work. Photograph courtesy of NASA

The Flight

After so many delays, it felt surrealistic to watch Artemis I launch on November 16. I woke up my wife, Julie, and 13-month-old daughter, Isabelle, to watch the SLS rocket take off at 00:47:44 Central Time. Tim and Brian were on console for our team, Randy and Sarah were getting ready to take over from them two hours after launch, and Colin and I were going to take the third shift several hours later.

I should have been asleep, but I didn't want to miss the historic launch, and I also wanted to find out what kind of day I was going to have. The SLS performed perfectly, and the TLI was perfect, so I was able to go to sleep with a positive feeling.

We supported the flight 24/7, with day, swing, and night shifts. Our team rotated through shifts, so no one was on any one shift the whole time (although Max had a lot of night shifts). Typically, two TARGOs were on console at a time, a prime and a second to help with the workload. We also rotated being prime and second. It was a rough schedule, particularly the first two-thirds of the mission where we not only supported on console, but spent time off-console cranking out off-nominal options for each mission phase based on the most up-to-date trajectory information.

So it was exhausting and a lot of work, but also fun and exciting. I loved getting to be in such a great seat to see this historic mission taking place and to be among so many hardworking and passionate experts who had dedicated so much of themselves to sending humans beyond low Earth orbit again. Even when I was sleep-deprived and waking up at odd hours, I was happy being in a place and time where I could do what I had dreamed about doing since I was nine years old. I'm sure many of the people there felt the same.

Throughout most of the mission, we talked over off-nominal options with the FDOs, did troubleshooting with the trajectories they were building, and performed additional analysis, like finding out if we could change our landing location after we had already left the Moon or finding our delay capability if we missed the Return Powered Flyby. Other teams in the MER asked us questions related to their own subsystems, some of which required analysis on our part. We also updated our console log so other TARGOs would know what had happened on previous shifts, and we had an hour at the beginning and end of each shift to perform the handover from the current team to the oncoming team (Figure 3).

Figure 3. Amelia Batcha, left, and Tim Dawn, center, in the process of handing over to Robert Harpold, right, when Orion was at its farthest distance from Earth. Photograph courtesy of NASA.

My personal highlight was being the prime TARGO on the shift where we performed the Outbound Powered Flyby. This burn took place near perilune, the closest approach to the Moon on the outbound leg of the trajectory, and would send us on a path so we could insert ourselves into the DRO. It was an exciting moment, because it was the point where we were returning a human-rated spacecraft to the Moon after 50 years.

The displays in the MER showed live video from the spacecraft, so when Max and I arrived for our shift that night, the Moon was starting to fill a substantial portion of the screen. Sarah, from whom we were taking over, gestured to the screen and said, "Welcome to the Moon."

Throughout the shift, the Moon kept getting larger and larger on the screen. Amelia joined us later to help with some of the work. The FDO and his backroom counterpart were setting up the spacecraft commands to perform the burn. Since the burn would be performed behind the Moon, we would lose contact for twenty minutes and wouldn't know if the burn was successful until the spacecraft reappeared from the other side. If the burn failed, we would regain contact with the spacecraft two minutes earlier. Both countdowns were displayed on the MER screens.

Up to the moment Orion went behind the Moon, everyone was checking their systems. The MER Manager announced we would have a go/no-go poll in a few minutes. It took me a second to realize what that meant, and I said it out loud to Max and Amelia: "Oh, wow, I get to be the one who says, 'Go!'"

When it came time for the poll, the MER Manager called, "TARGO?" I said, "Go!" maybe a little more forcefully than necessary. A few seconds later, the MER Manager repeated the question, and I realized I had spoken on the wrong loop. Even after all the training. I switched to the correct loop and said it again, with most of the enthusiasm of the first time.

On the screens, we could see Earth as a small blue ball. As the spacecraft got closer to passing behind the Moon, Earth moved closer and closer to the horizon. The final image before we lost contact showed the marble-sized Earth just above the Moon's horizon.

Once the spacecraft was out of contact, there was nothing we could do. People stood and started talking, and the atmosphere became festive. We'd gotten to the Moon! And Orion had taken some cool selfies with the Earth and Moon! (The title image for this article is one of those "selfies.") It was also a good time for restroom breaks. The MER Manager quieted us down two minutes before the first countdown, the one we didn't want to see, where the spacecraft would arrive early if it missed the burn.

That time came and went, and everyone felt relieved. Then, right on time, on the screens, we saw the Earthrise. Since the side of the Moon closest to Orion was unlit at that point, the view looked like Earth floating by itself in darkness. It was proof that OPF had been performed correctly, and that Orion was headed to the correct orbit. Everyone in the room clapped.

We remained busy for several days, performing three other major burns. After the RPF, Orion was locked on course toward its landing site on Earth, so there wasn't much the TARGOs could do. We kept supporting up to the shift before splashdown, doing occasional analysis and answering questions from other MER people.

I watched the splashdown from home. It was great seeing everything happen just as planned: the command and service modules separating, the spacecraft entering the atmosphere, the parachutes deploying, and the spacecraft landing in the water. After so many years, we had sent a human-rated spacecraft to the Moon, and it had performed extraordinarily well.

Next time, we're sending people there.

A Special Thank You!

We'd like to make Special Thank You to our Patreon Supporters at TIER Three and above. They each contribute at a monthly level that makes it possible for them to sponsor entire stories over time.

Thank you to Kelley Stead, Chewey, Eric Stallsworth, Candice Lisle, Jake Niehl, and Shanda Miller for providing the resources to publish "A Language Older than Words" by Andrew Giffin (One of our favorites in this issue!)

Daniel Antunes
Sponsor of
"Lost in Intuition"
by Amara Mesnik

Allan Seyberth
Sponsor of
"The Park"
by Teresa Mibrodt

Henry Gasko
Sponsor of
"Like Stars Daring to Shine"
by Somto Ihezue

Thank You

DREAMFORGE

Thank You to the DreamForge Magazine Team, without whom none of this would be possible:
Scot Noel, Editor-in-Chief
Jane Noel, Graphic Design, Layout & Social Media Support
Jane Lindskold, Senior Advisor & Creative Consultant
Catherine Weaver, Henry Gasko, Editorial Assistants
Lois Yeager, Copy Editor

Our profoundest thanks to Catherine Weaver and Henry Gasko who serve as our volunteer Editorial Assistants, and to Lois Yeager for her services as Copy Editor. Each have served selflessly to help us review and select stories, respond to submissions, and scour selected works for typos and grammatical glitches, making DreamForge as polished as it can be, and helping us continue to put out a great product.

Thanks also to all those who supported us financially each year through our Kickstarter and through regular Patreon support – especially our DreamCasters Writers Group. Your support provides the funds we need to buy great stories!

Thank you to the First Line Readers who helped us in selecting a wonderful range of stories for our issues this year, and for their exceptional dedication and passionate attention. In alphabetical order:

Mackenzie Autumn	Kelly Fox	Nicole Kosar
Storm Blakely	Henry Gasko	Anna Madden
Jarrid Cantway	N.V. Haskell	Jamie D. Munro
Daniel Cojocaru	Anja Hata	Jessica Rahden
Emily Dauvin	Todd Honeycutt	Indiana Tilford
Brandi Dixon	S.M. Isaac	Rachel Unger
Alecia Flores	Charles Kiley	Catherine Weaver
Rita Florez		

And Thank You to Our Founders

We bestow the honor of "Founder" on all those who subscribed to DreamForge (or pledged at the subcription levels on Kickstarter), either online or in print, before the end of February 2019. These are our treasured supporters who risked their dollars on a full year of DreamForge Magazine before we had a page in print to show for it.

Brynn Adams, Mike Adamson, Antha Ann Adkins, Virginia Altman, David Anderson, Tara-Jo Archer, Sean Arena, Lena Ariza, Freddie Avalos, Judith Avila, Fred Bailey, M. Michelle Bardon, Brandon Barkey, Barbara Barnett, Kim Barnett, Dagmar Baumann, Andrea Beneke, David Ben-Yaakov, Corona Berenices, Levi Biasco, Susan Biasco, Shawn Bilodeau, James Bing, Nicholas Boardman, Dennis Bolton, Ruth Bonanno, Lawrence Brandstetter, Ariel Brandt, Mike Breitkreutz, Samantha Bryant, Michael Burstein, Sarah Camargo, Rob Cameron, Connor Carbon, Chuck Cartia, Kylie Catlett, Paul Chiarulli, Michael Ciaraldi, Bruce Cloutier, Yvonne M. Coats, Lori Cochran, John Cocking, GMark Cole, Maurice Confer, John Cook, Phillip Coss, Ryan Coulombe, Caroline Couture, Stephen Cowan, Dave Cox, Peggy & Steve Cox, Dylan Craine, James Dailey, Cynthia Dalton, Amanda Davis, Evenstar Deane, Paul Dellinger, Aditya Deshmukh, Peter Donald, Heather Drinkwater, Laurie Dudasik, Scott Early, Jennifer Egri, Audrey Esquivel, Susan Estell, Andrew Evans, Richard & Ellen Farabaugh, Chrissy Feree, Alecia Flores, Adam Fout, Anthony Fox, Matt & Julia Frankle, Chad Freeman, Theresa Gage, Mark Gallacher, Anne Gibson, Allison Giordano, Rebecca Girash, Tammy Goodwin, John Goodwin (Galaxy Press), Philip Gorski, KC Grapes, Jason Grasty, Michele Graves, Paul Gray, Jaq Greenspon, Paul Grixti, Daniel & Sally W Grotta, James K Gruetzner, Gus Gyde, Phillip Hackney, Steven Halter, Dean Heller, Amanda Helling, Alea Henle, Fred Herman, Buddy Hernandez, Dennis Higbee, Alicia Hilton, Peter Hogg, Kylie Hogrefe, Tom Holmes, Todd Honeycutt, Saul Hymes, Keith Innes, Larry Ivkovich, Adnaňin Jašarevic, Heather Jesme, Erik Johnson, Fred Johnson, Brian Jovan, Commando Jugendstil, Jeremy Justus, Jack Keller, Gwendolyn Kelly, Annette Kennedy, Bruce Kennedy, Sean Killian, Shari Koseki, C. Aaron Kreader, Daniel Kuespert, Andrew Kuzneski, Brian Lambert, Nancy Lambert, Evergreen Lee, Mary Soon Lee, Robert Lee, Keith Leonard, Corey Leverette, Niv Levy, Anita Libby, Jane Lindskold, Kyle Linn, Cecilia Lins-Morstadt, Darren Lipman, Adam Lippmann, David Locke, Richard Lopez, Connor Louiselle, Joel Lovell, Jefferson Lowrey, Matthew Luce, Anna Madden, Ralph Mazza, Drew McCaffrey, Michael McCormick, Rachael McCormick, Nancy McDonald, Terry McGarry, Jamie McMenamy, Emerson McNerney, Mark Meadows, Clinton Medbery, Kestrel Michaud, Kim Milburn, Lee-Anne Miles, Eric Mitchell, Olivia Montoya, James Moore, Matthew Moran, Mab Morris, Paul Motsuk, Patricia Moussatche, Bruce Moxley, Jamie D. Munro, Ann Nalley, Pam Newberry, Emily Newman, Kaleb Nichols, Christopher Niessl, Paul Norwood, Fiona Nowling, Brian Nutwell, James T. O'Donnell, Richard Ohnemus, Eric Pansen, Kate Parr, Nancy Passaflora, Nick Payne, Barbara Peterson, Danene Peterson, Heidi Pilewski, Tom Pollard, Drum Priest, David Ranf, Magnus Redgrove, David Rhode, Felicia Richards, Jodi Rizzotto, Timothy Robey, Alberto Romano, Angela Rose O'Brien, Les Rosenthal (Sci Fi Saturday Night), Nate Russell, Joy Sabl, Sulaimaan Salim, Gregory Scheckler, Bjoern Schneider, Frank Schurter, Larry Schwartz, Andrew Searls, Robert Seres, Tracy Smith, Allen Snyder, Tor Solli-Nowlan, Nate Stephens, Eston Stiles, Ian Stoffel, Graham Stone, Lucy Stone, Christopher Straka, Lif Strand, Susan Stripay, Hugh & Mary Swearman, Laurie Sweeney, Frank Terwilliger, Emily Tippetts, Kima Traynham, Christian Turner, Sarena Ulibarri, Jaap van Poelgeest, Stephen Vater, James Verran, Mark Visconti, KL Wagoner, Angie Watts, Christopher Weeks, Matthew Welch, Dave Wells, Doctor Who10, Karen Widmaier, Alicyn Wierdrich, Nick Williams, Andrew Wilson, John Winkelman, Sean Winnie, Cliff Winnig, Bobbi Wolf, Donald Wuenschell, Kevin Yeager, Lois Yeager, Russell & Dorothy Yeager, Robert Zamarron, Hal Zhang, Dark Regions Press, The Dome

CONNECTING DREAMERS - PAST AND FUTURE
IMAGINE • ENGAGE • INSPIRE